ALSO BY ROBLEY WILSON, JR.

Short fiction

THE PLEASURES OF MANHOOD (1977)
LIVING ALONE (1978)
DANCING FOR MEN (1983)

Poetry

KINGDOMS OF THE ORDINARY (1987)

Terrible Kisses

Stories

ROBLEY WILSON, JR.

Simon and Schuster

NEW YORK   LONDON   TORONTO   SYDNEY   TOKYO

Simon and Schuster
Simon & Schuster Building
Rockefeller Center
1230 Avenue of the Americas
New York, New York 10020

SIMON AND SCHUSTER and colophon are registered trademarks of Simon & Schuster Inc.
Manufactured in the United States of America
1   3   5   7   9   10   8   6   4   2
Library of Congress Cataloging-in-Publication Data
Wilson, Robley.
Terrible kisses: stories/Robley Wilson, Jr.
p.   cm.
Fourteen stories originally published 1985–1988.
I. Title.
PS3573.I4665T4   1989
813'.54—dc19   89-31179
CIP
ISBN 0-671-67919-8

"Africa" was first published in *TriQuarterly*, "Feature Presentations" and "Payment in Kind" in *Sewanee Review*, and "Sons" in *The American Voice*. "Favorites" was published originally in *Stories About Things That Fall Apart, and What Happens When They Do* (Word Beat Press, 1985). "Cats" first appeared in *The New Yorker*; "Silent Partners" in *The Cream City Review*; "Nam" in *The Georgia Review*; "Praises" in *The Laurel Review*, and "The Eventual Nuclear Destruction of Cheyenne, Wyoming" in *The Atlantic*. "Sisters" was a selection of the PEN Syndicated Fiction Project (1988). "Payment in Kind" was reprinted in *New American Short Stories* (New American Library, 1987).

Acknowledgments

Completion of this collection was made possible by a fellowship from the John Simon Guggenheim Foundation and by a Professional Development Leave from the University of Northern Iowa.

"*Now I know how prolific Nature is—wasteful, prodigal,
extravagant—how infinitely productive. That's what genius
is. What's efficiency to God? Nature will try anything.
Look at evolution. Look at the stars. Look at damned cancer.
"The good news is: Nothing is ever finished, and nothing
is ever enough—and so you cannot stop being a painter, though
you think you've no pictures left, and I cannot stop being a
writer, though I've no time left. . . . "*
—from "Praises"

Contents

Terrible Kisses

Africa

Married, childless, nearly sixty years old, Seth Sharp lived now where he had lived all his life, in a weathered house in New Hampshire, close by a green and oval lake, in sight on clear days of the Presidential Range of the White Mountains. It was gray, small, a frame cottage with shutters painted dirty red; it was two miles from a gravel road, three miles from the nearest neighbor, thirteen miles from the town of Adams. It faced northwest, took the slant light of the afternoon sun, and it was a place that suited Seth almost entirely.

Except it had never had a porch—not in the time of his parents, nor even in the time of his well-off grandparents— and Seth burned with a secret sense of deprivation. He had told his wife, when he married her and brought her to this house:

"You wait and see. I'll have a nice porch on this place."

And his wife, Agatha, had kissed him and smiled, and gone

about the business of cleaning up the single bedroom so the two of them might lie respectably together.

Twenty years later he had not built the porch, but he went on promising himself he would. And to his wife:

"Aggie, next spring I am dead sure to fasten a porch onto this place."

Long winter evenings when the snow sighed outside the windows, Seth sat curled on the horsehair sofa close up to a kerosene lamp and used the fat family Bible for a desk under his sketches. He drew and erased, and wrote and scratched out, and built up hazardous structures on the yellow paper under his pencils. Over the years, the porch of his plans began to look more and more like the porch in his mind. He said to his wife:

"Aggie, this is the year I'm going to build her."

He was tired of having no place to sit watching the progress of the seasons, no place to put a rocking chair in the evenings, no place to puff on his pipe or breathe the woodsy air or ponder Mt. Washington on clear days.

This year, on Thursday of the first week in August, Seth drove into Adams in his pickup, showed his sketches to the dealer at the lumberyard, and drove home at indecent speed with more than four hundred dollars' worth of lumber and tar paper piled in the truck bed. It represented all he and Aggie had managed to save throughout their marriage, and if it was not enough, it was as much as he could afford. He began work immediately—though the sun had already dropped behind the mountains and shade had turned the surrounding woods cold—and succeeded in framing his porch before impossible darkness set in. At dawn the next day he threw himself out of his respectable bed, gulped a cup of thick coffee, and resumed his labors.

By working all day, he was able to finish nailing in the floor joists; Saturday he laid the one-by-sixes of the flooring; Sunday he nailed the roof together and covered it with the tar paper. He had his porch at last. It needed only steps.

That evening, while the sun still balanced at the summit of the nearest mountain, he commanded Aggie to help him drag the parlor sofa onto his porch so the two of them could sit and watch the coming of the night. Long after she had gone to bed, Seth sat on in the summer darkness, admiring the moonstruck treetops over the orange bowl of his pipe. Next morning, when he helped his wife move the sofa, spongy with dew, back into the house, he decided he would have to think about real porch furniture—chairs with thin metal legs, and perhaps one of those flimsy lounges with webbed seats and backs.

All day Monday he paced the length and breadth of the porch like a man measuring off the plot of ground for a garden or a grave. In between these tours, he leaped down from the porch and admired it from a distance. Then he clambered back up and resumed his pacing. From every angle Seth took in his porch with a child's smile and a gaze of innocent respect, as if he could not quite believe his own hands capable of such a masterpiece. It had yet to be painted, and because it had no steps his wife was obliged to use only the back door, but it was a possession of his own, an extension eight feet deep and fifteen wide of his personal vision of the world; the worthiest of his ancestors had not owned such a property. He would not let the cat sleep on it, he would not let Aggie walk on it unless he was with her, and he talked of it incessantly.

"I intend to close up the front and sides with those real thin little slats," he told his wife. "I seen 'em at Murdoch's last month, all criss-cross in the brochure. I'll paint the slats red to match the shutters, and the floor I'll use good deck paint on, and a good grade of house paint on the rest of it. Nothing cheap."

Then he went to the Bible and drew a sheet of yellow paper from inside the cover.

"I'm working on that pair of steps, too," he said. "They're tricky, but don't you worry."

Agatha smiled and went out the back to get to her rock garden in front of the house. She did not remind him the porch roof might want shingles; the roof was the one part of his handiwork he could not see.

Seth found a pencil and returned to his labors, less artistic than mathematical at this late stage. When his wife stopped on her way to bed, to kiss him on top of the head and steal a glance at his work, she saw a much-smeared page crowded with fractions tentatively subtracted around the geometry of his steps. He looked up at her, confident.

"Don't you worry," he said, and bowed again over the Bible.

It was nearly midnight when he folded the yellow paper in half and tucked it back inside the cover of the book. Before he joined Aggie in their bed he strolled out to the porch one last time, standing at the edge of it where the steps would be, and urinated off it to the pine-needled ground. Just for a few moments Seth realized how deep the pleasure of life could be. He gave a little jump; if the porch was not truly rock-solid, at least it did not give way. He leaned against a roof support; it felt cool against his palm. A railing. He would build a railing, too, both for appearance and strength. He took a deep breath, letting the mingled odors of pine forest, pine lumber, and pungent urine make him giddy and happy.

Undressing, slipping into bed beside his wife, he realized his lips were moving. He caught himself and smiled. Here in the dark he had been looking up at the ceiling, saying, over and over, "Thank you, thank you, thank you."

He had no idea how many hours had passed when he woke up and heard rain, and for several long minutes he lay still and listened through the opened bedroom window to the sounds of the storm. It was a heavy, steady downpour, filling

the woods around the house with a noise like the wind, drumming on the roof, shattering the blackness every so often with
a lightning flash. The thunder came after, gradually closer
and louder; Seth imagined it was the thunder that had jogged
him out of sleep. At first he thought he would simply roll
over—perhaps put an arm around Aggie to secure himself to
the comfort of reality—and drift back into whatever quiet
place he had just come from. Then he knew he was not
sleepy, and that what he most wanted was to get out of bed
and walk on the new porch, to enjoy this summer rainstorm
from a vantage he had never had until now.

He sat up and swung his thin legs over the side of the bed.
The floor under his feet was damp and cool; the light breeze
that came into the room through the window washed lightly
over his nakedness. He felt refreshed—because he had slept
and because the touch of the cleansed air was invigorating—
and the happiness he had hugged in his sleep came flooding
back to him.

"By damn," he said, and was startled to hear the words. He
had meant only to think them; the whisper of them in the
room was a thought made actual, as if he had created something out of nothing. But of course he had done exactly that.

His wife stirred, moaned in her sleep as he stood and made
his way gingerly across the bedroom toward the kitchen.
When a flicker of lightning showed him the opened doorway
he moved more quickly, crossed the kitchen, and stood for a
few moments at the screen door. The odor of fresh lumber
filled his nostrils, widened his smile. The wetness of the rain
intensified the odor, deepened it; it was as if the wood were
returning to forest, growing branches and spills, recovering its
pine-ness and insisting its immortality. The notion pleased
Seth. At the very least, the porch would outlast him, outlast
Aggie; it would be a legacy for any man who might buy this
place thirty or forty years from now. He felt proud—and even
understood how rare the feeling was.

He was about to step outside, to stroll the length of the

porch in his bare feet, when a sound arrested him, froze him.
It sounded like a moan, or a sob, or both—the sound a
woman might make in her sleep. He listened. When it came
again he was not sure it was a woman; it might have been an
animal noise, but it was not from the surrounding woods. It
was close. It seemed to be on the porch—there it was again
—and now it was accompanied by a thumping, something
striking the porch floor, scraping across it. Seth pushed at the
door and peered out.

Nothing. Darkness. No, shadows that flickered against the
trees and danced with the falling rain. He squinted, listened.
Stepped out. Had he heard only the creaking of the trees, and
water dripping from the eaves? He walked to the edge of the
porch. Lightning flashed; it made him blink and silhouetted
the treetops in front of the cottage. The thunderclap made
him blink again, and it was only as he felt the floor under him
tremble from the shock of the thunder that he remembered
he had seen something strange in the brilliance of the light.
Something on his porch. Someone.

Whoever it was lay close by the wall of the house, and Seth
moved warily toward what he had seen. Now he thought it
was a man.

"Who is it?" he said. Then, realizing he had whispered, he
talked up: "Who in hell is out here?"

He got no answer. Let me have another splash of lightning,
he thought. And it came—this time dangerously close and
blinding, the thunder right on top of it and a smell like a
burnt-out motor filling the air. Seth's voice rose out of the
noise like a different and more potent thunder:

"What is it you think you're doing?"

It was a couple, a man and a woman, and they were
wrapped in each other's arms, bodies indecent, locked in
what had to be lovemaking. Both were half-undressed, a piece
of the woman's clothing caught at one of her ankles, the
man's trousers pulled down to discover his bare thighs.

"Jesus H. and John R. Christ!" Seth shrieked. In the restored darkness he stumbled toward the two, his fists clenched, kicking and cursing. It made no difference that he was barefoot, that he was more naked than they. He stood over them, kicking with both feet, hoping to hurt them more than he hurt himself. He kicked them in the direction of the near end of the porch.

"Get off!" he yelled. "Get-goddamn-off-this-goddamn-porch!"

They came apart, like the two halves of something broken, and scrambled ahead of him on hands and knees. The woman covered herself; her underwear—if that was what he'd seen—she abandoned as she tried to avoid his feet. He caught up to her over and over again, punishing her belly, her legs. The man was yanking up his pants, trying to stand, trying to talk.

"Wait a minute," he was saying. "Hold on a minute, damn it."

The words were broken. Seth punctuated them with kicks, with the closed fists he was using to pummel the man.

"Get off! Get off! Get off!"

The man, whoever he was, jumped when he got to the end of the porch—vaulted to the ground, then came back to the woman, but by that time Seth had already seized her arms, hauling her halfway to her feet and wrestling her off the porch. She gasped when she landed, the wind knocked out of her. Seth stood looking down at them.

"And don't come back. I catch you doing that stuff on my property again, I'll shoot you both." He knew there was an old shotgun somewhere in the closet behind the bedroom; he thought it might still fire. "Go on; get gone!"

Lightning gave him a last glimpse of them: the man pale, his hair slicked over his forehead by the downpour; the woman half-standing, supported by her lover as if she could not stay upright by herself, her mouth open to show the whiteness of her teeth, her long hair heavy with the rain. Seth watched them move away, the man helping the woman in the direction of the woods. Satisfied that he had repulsed them, he turned on his heel, picked up the scrap of woman's clothing that felt slippery in his fingers, and went into the house. Outrage had stiffened his muscles, his spine. He ached with it, hurt from it. From under the kitchen sink he drew out the bottle of bourbon Aggie kept for medicinal purposes and took a long, harsh swallow. It was like a bad dream: two filthy-minded strangers defiling his new porch.

"I'll be damned," he said out loud. The experience had so shaken him, he took a second swallow. Summer people, he thought, camping in the woods. Probably the rain had soaked their tent, dripped through onto their sleeping bag, driven them out to find new shelter. He studied the woman's under-pants—shiny-white, lacy. All wet and hot and horny, he thought; what a hell of a place to pick to go at each other.

He laid the garment on the table beside the Bible. Then he took a last swig from the bottle and went back to bed.

He had scarcely crossed the muddled border of sleep when he was once more dragged back to wakefulness. He sat upright in the bed; the house clattered with violent hammerings at the screen door. A voice was calling, small behind the fists, but frantic.

"In there!" the voice cried. "In there! You! Wake up in there!"

Agatha stirred beside him. On her stomach, she raised herself to her elbows, her forehead damp against Seth's shoulder.

"What is it?" she said.

Seth shook his head, meaning ignorance, waking up. Then, as if he were possessed, he flung the sheet aside and jumped to the floor.

"That horny goat," he said; he nearly choked on the words. "He's back again." He was already at the bedroom door, turned up the lamp on the dresser, bolted naked into the kitchen.

"Make yourself decent," his wife cried. She got out of bed.

"I'll show him decent," Seth screamed, while the banging went on so loud the voices inside and out were lost in the echo of it. Behind him, Agatha raised the kerosene lamp.

"Fetch that old shotgun out of the closet," Seth ordered.

He flung open the door. For an instant the scene was a tableau: of Agatha, her hair stringy and disheveled, looking frightened and small in a blue cotton housecoat dusted over with a print of yellow flowers; of Seth, his stark white skin hollowed between his shoulder blades and puffy over his buttocks, crouched to defend the sanctity of his porch a second time; and of a stocky, fortyish man caught in the gold of the lamplight, his eyes wild, his round face running with rain and sweat.

It was Agatha who set time moving again.

"It's Raymond," she whispered.

"What?" said Seth. He was still crouched, still ghostly simian.

"It's Raymond. It's my brother." She began walking toward the door, taking short, hesitant steps in her bare feet. "It's little brother Raymond."

Seth straightened up. "I'll be goddamned," he said.

The man lifted his arms toward the lamplight, opening his hands to his sister.

"Ag," he said hoarsely, "Ag, help us. Help her."

Agatha ran past him to the porch. The two men faced each other in the shadowy kitchen: Raymond clenching his fists, Seth open-mouthed, swaying between sleep and fierce wakefulness.

"Was that you out there before?" Seth said. "Out there going at it with that woman?"

"It was me."

Seth blinked. "I ain't seen you in twenty years," he said. "I thought you was in New Orleans or Dallas or someplace like that."

"You could have killed her," Raymond said. "Kicking her like that. We think she might be pregnant."

Agatha stood in the doorway. "There's a girl out here," she told her husband. "The poor thing looks barely alive."

Raymond raised one arm to point at Seth. "He did it."

Seth shook his head. "Hell, I didn't even have shoes on. I couldn't of done her any harm if I'd wanted to."

"Well, help me," Agatha said.

"I'll help." Raymond followed his sister to the porch.

Seth pulled a straight chair out from the table and sat, muddled. The caning was sharp on his buttocks, but he didn't need to get dressed to see what was going to happen next. He wondered if he should fetch the shotgun himself, since Aggie had ignored his earlier command. Montgomery or Biloxi or Little Rock—Raymond had gone somewhere south back in the nineteen-sixties. What in hell was he doing up here in New Hampshire, lying on Seth's porch in the rain, on top of some knocked-up girl Aggie looked worried about?

Now there was more commotion at the door. Raymond's back appeared; the arms of the hurt woman dangled on either side of him as he came into the kitchen with short, shuffling steps. Then here was Aggie at the other end, holding the girl by the ankles while Raymond supported her under the shoulders. The girl looked to be unconscious.

"I never even wore shoes," Seth repeated.

"He flung her off the porch, like she was some kind of animal. She fell on all those rocks."

"Take her straight into the bedroom," Agatha said, "all the way back past the stove there." It was if she had no interest in what had already happened, but only in what might happen next.

"You going to put her in our bed?" Seth said. He watched them pass. The woman was limp as a rag, eyes shut, head lolled to one side. Her clothes were muddy and rumpled. She was dark-skinned. Seth got to his feet.

"Hey," he said. "That's a colored girl." No one responded

to him. He trailed after Agatha toward the bedroom, his right
hand held out as if to take her attention. "Hey," he said to
her back.

"Not now," she told him. She vanished into the bedroom;
Seth stood outside the door.

"You going to put a colored in my bed? In our bed?" He
heard the sound of springs, of linens pulled aside, of the
exertions of Raymond and Aggie arranging their patient. He
turned back into the kitchen and sat heavily in the caned
chair. It made no sense—none of it. Seth knew what his
mother would have said, God rest her, if she were on hand.

"It ain't proper, Aggie," he said.

She appeared in the doorway. "Heat some water," she told
him, "and find me some clean towels."

He brought water up into the pump alongside the kitchen
sink and filled the copper kettle. None of the towns he'd
worked in—and he'd worked in five or six New Hampshire
towns before marrying and settling down with Aggie—none
had a single colored family in them. He set the kettle on the
stovetop, rattled the grate, opened the damper to make
higher heat. The alarm clock on the stove shelf over his head
read five o'clock. Five o'clock in the morning; the time startled him.

"Jesus," he said under his breath. He sat down to wait for
the water to boil.

Raymond came out of the bedroom.

"Where are those clean towels?" he said.

"Keep your shirt on," Seth said. "I'm trying to think where
she keeps the damned things." He got up and padded across
the kitchen to the sideboard. "I don't know if she wants dish
towels or hand towels."

"Hand towels." Agatha stood just inside the kitchen.
"Give me a couple of those big white ones in the bottom
drawer."

Seth stooped over the drawer and brought out the towels.
"How come we never use these?" he said.

"Because they're for company." She took them from him. "That's how it happens they're not worn out like everything else we own."

"That trash is no company," Seth said. He went back to sit at the kitchen table. The shiny underwear lay near his hand; he picked it up and fondled it.

"Why don't you put some clothes on," Agatha said. "And I don't mean those flimsy panties."

"I'll dress when I feel like it." He tossed the underpants aside. To Raymond, who had come to sit down at the other side of the table, he said, "How the dickens did a smart guy like you get tied up with a nigger?"

"She's mulatto," Raymond said. "And don't use that word around me."

"What's mulatto?"

"She's not all Negro."

"There never was one of them people all Negro, to hear them tell it." He looked at his wife, who made motions with her hands for him to stop talking. "I recollect an old nigger used to pick up beer and tonic bottles out on the Rochester road. Black as under your fingernails. He was always telling folks how he was part white—one quarter or one twentieth or one ninety-ninth. Some outlandish fraction a man couldn't take a peck of to total up to the number one. They all got that story down by heart."

"This is no story," Raymond said coolly. "Lana's half white."

"What's that name?"

"Lana. Lana Turner Windham."

Seth sat back in his chair. He looked at Agatha, then at her brother.

"I'll be goddamned," he said. "I'll be god-double-damned." He stood up, walked across the kitchen, and looked into the dim room where the girl was sleeping. Then he came back to the table.

"I got to say it," he told his brother-in-law, "that you are a

far sight dumber than any man who talks good ought to be, if
you believe that nigger girl is any bit whiter than two ton of
the Adams Coal Company's bituminous."

"I said she's half white. I didn't say she wasn't Negro."

"I guess you figure her name makes her half white," Seth
said gleefully. "I guess if I changed my name to Booker T.
Washington Sharp, you'd tell it around that I was half nigger." He giggled and slapped the cover of the old Bible so
hard the dust flew.

"Listen," Raymond said. The blood had gone out of his
face, and the force of his gripping the table turned his thumbs
flour-colored. "I told you I don't like that word 'nigger.' "

"You listen!" Seth interrupted. "You listen! Nigger nigger
nigger nigger nigger!" He shouted the word, dropping each 'r'
so that what resounded in the small kitchen was like gibber-
ish.

Raymond got to his feet, but Seth tasted rage as bitter as
before; he went on shouting. "And while you was filthying up
my new porch last night, tell me which part of that half-
nigger did you think was white? The part you was plumbing?"

His brother-in-law was moving around the table toward
him. Agatha stood, petrified, in front of the stove. Seth
backed slowly toward the wall.

"Now I want you to get off this property and take your girl
with you. If she's so white as you say she is, I ain't going to
have that shoe polish she puts on to look like a nigger come
rubbing off on the sheets and making laundry work for my old
lady." He stopped, his back fast against the wall and no place
to go. "Don't you come near me!" he shrieked. "Don't you
lay a hand on me!"

Raymond had gripped him by the shoulder with one hand,
and struck him across the face with the closed fist of the
other.

It was a stupendous blow; it caught Seth on the cheek and
it set off geysers of broken color inside his eyelids. He slid
down the wall to the floor, and with his hands, which had

gone cold as ice, he felt the floorboards tilt up to stand parallel with his naked body. He pushed the floor back to horizontal and sat numbly, moving his head from side to side.

"There was no call to do that," he mumbled. He opened his eyes and looked up warily. Raymond was standing over him, fists still cocked. Agatha was leaning against the stove. Neither made a move to comfort him where he sat.

"I am not going to move that girl," Raymond said, "because I don't know how badly you hurt her. I saved her life in Mississippi, and I don't intend for her to be killed in New Hampshire."

Seth stared at the floor. "I ain't keen on minding any pregnant coloreds in my house," he said sullenly.

"I'll pay you for the room, and for what food she eats."

"There's things that bother me a sight more than money."

He watched his brother-in-law kneel in front of him, his big fist hovering an inch from Seth's eyes.

"Now you attend to me," Raymond said. "I'm going into town for help, and if that girl is any worse when I come back, I will beat you within a half-inch of your scrawny life. You hear?"

Seth kept quiet, listening only to the throbbing in his head.

"And if she should by any chance die because of how you kicked her," Raymond went on grimly, "or if she miscarries, I will kill you with my bare hands. You hear that?"

Seth nodded. Raymond stood up and turned away from him.

"Are you going to fetch a doctor?" Agatha said.

"Yes."

"And a minister, too?"

Her brother almost smiled. "You want a wedding?" Raymond put his arm around her shoulders, touched her forehead with a brief kiss.

"If the baby belongs to you," his sister said. "And if you're not man and wife already."

He gave her a long, fond look. "That would make you happy," he said.

Agatha beamed.

"I'd hate to tell you how long my people have lived in this state of New Hampshire," Seth said. "It's a sight longer than there's been niggers in Mississippi; I'm damn sure about that. As long as there's been niggers in Africa, maybe."

Raymond stopped at the door and said, "I don't know what that's supposed to mean." He glared at Seth, his teeth working nervously over his lower lip.

Seth shrugged and used the back of the kitchen chair to pull himself to his feet. "I guess nothing," he said dully.

He watched Raymond get down from the new porch and walk in the growing daylight straight to the pickup. Seth swore at himself for leaving the key in the ignition, cursed Raymond as the truck drove off toward town. LIVE FREE OR DIE, read the slogan on the license plate.

"I hope you're satisfied," Aggie said. "Fighting with your own kin."

"Your kin, not mine," Seth said. "Stealing. Fornicating. Turning against Nature."

"Go cover yourself," she said. "I declare it mystifies me, how your mind works."

All morning Agatha kept a close eye on him. When she worked outside—weeding the vegetables in the clearing beyond the outhouse, or transplanting hens and chickens in the rock garden—she asked him to keep her company, even though she could not oblige him to help with her chores. When she was inside, at the stove or the sink, he felt her looking at him over her shoulder as he sat at the kitchen table and scribbled step calculations or went through the motions of cleaning his pipe. If she went to do something in the parlor, she was back in no time.

"Just what is it you're scared of?" he said once. "Do you think I'd dirty myself?"

When she was through with her planting and cleaning, and after she had warmed up the franks and beans from Saturday's supper for Seth, Agatha sat for a while beside Raymond's Lana. Seth kept his distance, as deliberate and uninterested as he could pretend to be. In mid-afternoon Agatha went into the parlor and sat on the sofa with a basket of sewing. Seth watched, dividing his attention between the yellow paper—though he had done nothing new with the sketches for his porch steps; it was all a sham—and his wife. He could see that she kept looking out the window, hoping for Raymond to appear. Maybe Raymond couldn't find a doctor who'd treat a colored person. Maybe Raymond was all talk, and wouldn't even come back. He watched Aggie's face, watched her eyes, watched her hands slow over the sewing.

When she dozed, her head resting against the back of the horsehair sofa, Seth waited several minutes to be sure, then tiptoed to the doorway of Lana's bedroom. The girl, too, was asleep—at least, she had her eyes closed—and unaware of him. Now that he saw her in the light she seemed younger than he had guessed she was. Twenty-five, he thought. Thirty at the most. And pretty, if you thought those people could be pretty with their thick lips and monkey bones. Yet she was not nearly so dark as he'd remembered, not so dark as he'd pictured her while he and Raymond had argued in the kitchen a few hours earlier. Lana Turner Windham was quite light, in fact—almost like a white girl who spent a lot of time in the sun. Her hands—the palms of them—would actually be white; Seth knew that. And the soles of her feet. Not bad. Maybe Raymond knew what he was doing; maybe it was true that those people had some special and secret knowledge about sex. He took a step into the room. A board creaked; the girl's eyes opened and fixed on him.

"What d'you want?" she said.

Seth stared at her. The brown skin made her eyes look

enormous. "I just wanted to ask you something," he lied. What could she really know that Seth didn't?

"Ask," she told him.

"I wondered if it was true."

"If what was true?"

"Is it true you're pregnant from Ray."

"I maybe am," she said. "We're not sure. I'm maybe only late, or skipped."

"What color will it be?" Seth said. Now he realized he was staring at her—at a bruise on her face, just under her left eye —and lowered his eyes to her hands outside the bed sheet.

"What kind of question is that?"

"Will it be black? Will it be white? It's an easy question. Will it be something like coffee regular, part milk and part java?"

"I don't know," she said. She turned her face into the pillow—his and Aggie's pillow—and closed her eyes, as if to make him vanish.

"I don't think you're pregnant anyhow," Seth said.

"I told you," the girl said. "I'm maybe not."

"Is it true Ray saved you from being killed?"

"Yes." She said it into the pillow.

Seth hesitated; he had never met anybody who was alive because of somebody else. Then he said: "How'd he do it?"

"I don't know."

"How come you don't know? Are you stupid?"

She turned her face out of the linens. "I was real small," she said. "And no, I am not stupid."

"How old are you?"

"I'm twenty-four."

"How old were you when Ray saved your life?"

"Five years old, maybe. Or six."

Seth stared at her for several moments, sizing her up, weighing and rejecting more questions. She met his gaze coolly, squarely.

"When's the first time he took you to bed?" Seth said.

"That's his business and mine."

Seth sneered. "Monkey business," he said.

"Get out of my room," the girl said.

"It's my room," he said, "and like hell I will."

"Then shut your mouth and let me sleep." She rolled onto her stomach and pulled the pillow over her head.

"Bitch," Seth said.

Her movement had left her partly uncovered. He gazed at her bare back, at the straps of her bra—the thin verticals and the broader horizontal band of white cloth. The garment was stark against her brown skin. He thought about Raymond undressing Lana Windham whenever he felt like it. He thought of Raymond on top of her on the new porch. The two images swam in his head in a confusion of envy and anger.

"Bitch," he repeated.

He went out to the kitchen and sat at the table, where the bottle of whiskey, the Bible, and the hurt girl's underwear were still arranged like objects in a painting. He knew if he opened the Bible to the proper chapters he would find an anger to equal his own, and a promise of vengeance from the same God who punished Sodom and Gomorrah—a God whose Justice was every whit as complex and mathematical as the correct design for the porch steps. Damned fornicators, he and God would say in unison. Trespassers. Unnatural couple. They had stolen all the pleasure the porch had given him, had upset his work on the steps. He wanted to wake Agatha, shake her off the parlor sofa as if his fury could jolt her into helping him get things back to normal. Send your damned brother back to wherever, he wanted to say. You and me, we never had any trouble by ourselves. Now we've got nothing but. Monkey-girl. Goat-man. Two freaks making a circus out of a good life.

"Old man?"

Seth turned in the chair. Monkey-girl. Lana stood unsteadily in the bedroom doorway, draped in a white sheet from her shoulders to her ankles.

"What in the hell do you want now?" he said.

"I don't feel so good. Where's your bathroom?"

He stared at her.

"What's the matter?" she said. "Haven't you got one?"

"We got one," Seth said. "I thought your kind went in the woods, like apes."

"Hey," she said, "just tell me where it is."

He gestured toward the back door. "Outside," he said. "In back."

She grimaced. "Sounds to me like you-all's the ones go in the woods." She started unsteadily toward the door.

"What's the matter with you?" Seth said.

She stopped. "What do you care?"

"I don't," he said. "Why'n't you and Raymond tell us you was coming here?"

Lana looked around the room. "I don't see you got any telephone," she said.

"You could of written. Or maybe you can't."

"Ray wanted to surprise his sister."

"I'll say it was a surprise. Dirtying my new porch . . ."

"The idea was we'd wait until you and your wife woke up. We didn't want to disturb you at no three in the morning. We started off just sitting out of the rain. The rest of it—it kind of happened."

Seth closed his eyes, saw the two of them all over again. Disgust churned in him. Animals, he reminded himself.

"If you don't mind," Lana said, "I'll just go on to your outhouse." She paused, the door half-opened and the afternoon sun lighting her young face, touching the bruise on her cheek with dull color. "No electric," she said, "no plumbing, no telephone. We never lived this uncivilized since I was a little kid."

The door slapped shut, cutting off whatever hard answer Seth might have made up, and he sat, dumb, at the table. What ran through his thoughts showed on his face. The possibility of following her—of tearing away the sheet and wrestling her into the bushes, teaching her what-for. Trapping her

inside the privy, locking the door from outside; let her stay
there a while, breathing the decay odors, getting scared. How
come you smell so bad? Raymond would say to her. Or finding
a crack in the privy where he could spy in, watch her do what
she was doing—see what she looked like in that white bra
and no underpants, see what Raymond saw. Uncivilized! He
could wait outside for her, knock her down, finish what he'd
started on the porch. How do you like this? And this? I may
not have much, but I don't have a dead monkey inside me.

Seth stood up from the table. He was giddy from thinking
what he might do to Lana Windham, and the giddiness carried him like a drunkard into the bedroom where she had
lain. The bed was a rumple of linens—the top sheet gone,
the blanket thrown against the footboard, the two pillows
pushed against the head. He could see the impression of her
small body on the bottom sheet, could imagine her as he had
seen her earlier, the white straps of the bra thin as string
against her dark skin. Seth yanked at the blanket and flung it
to the floor, pulled the sheet off the mattress, caught one
pillow as it tumbled after the sheet and threw it toward the
door that led back to the kitchen. Bitch! he thought. He
kicked the bedclothes out from underfoot and went to the
closet.

In the back right corner he found it: a 12-gauge shotgun
Agatha's father had given him thirty years before. He hauled
it out into the light, took it in his right hand, rested the twin
barrels across his left arm. It was unexpectedly heavy; the
barrels were touched with patches of dark orange rust, and
the varnished stock showed mildew like flower petals. He had
never fired the gun—had not hunted with it, had not had to
defend himself with it. Until today, he could not have imagined a use for it.

He managed to break the gun open and peered into the
breech; it wasn't loaded. That was all right. In a kitchen
drawer there had used to be a box of shells and a narrow
yellow carton of cleaning materials, and probably they were

still there. That might come later. For now, he hurried out of the bedroom, trampling the linens, anxious to be at the back door before Raymond's concubine got there. Uncivilized! Perhaps he would use the gun like a club, raise it again and again until the girl couldn't get up, or perhaps he would only enjoy seeing her terrified, making her beg for mercy, listening to her promise him anything—anything—if he would let her go.

He met her halfway between the back door and the end of the path.

"You stop there," he said. "Nigger bitch."

"What's the matter with you?" she said. She hugged the sheet tight around her and stared—seemed to marvel—at the gun pointed toward her. "You crazy?"

"I want you off my property," Seth said. His mouth tasted bitter, like stale coffee. "I want you back where you came from."

"Are you going to murder me?"

"I might," he said, knowing he couldn't unless he went back to the kitchen and found the shotgun shells. "I might murder you."

She stood, swaying, watching him. She was about ten feet from him—too far to reach out and try to twist the gun out of his hands. Now would be the time she could unwrap the sheet, show herself to him, say: Look at this. Don't you want this? Now would be the time for her at least to get down on her knees and beg.

"You stupid old man," she said.

He tightened his grip on the shotgun and gestured with it toward the road, out of sight on the other side of the house.

"Get off this property," he repeated. "You're downgrading the place, making it cheap. I already got to burn your bedclothes."

"You stupid, crazy old man," Lana said. "Ray'll come back and get you good."

"I'll look out for him," he said.

"Where's my clothes?"

"You don't need clothes. Your kind don't."

She took a new grip on the sheet, careful for it not to tangle her legs. "I'll get gone," she said. "You aren't fit to kill me, old man."

"I'll see you get safe to the road," Seth said. "I'll be right behind you."

"Maybe you ought to see this first," she said. She opened the sheet so he could see her bare legs. She's doing it, Seth thought; she's offering herself. But then he saw, and his stomach turned. Blood was what she showed him—dark and dried on the inside of her legs where she had tried to wipe it away, glistening red where it was fresh on her thighs.

"What did you do to yourself?" he said hoarsely.

Lana did a clumsy pirouette, flouncing the sheet at him. "Nothing," she said. "But there's no more baby here."

Agatha was hard to rouse. When he spoke her name she barely stirred; he had to take her by the arm and shake her. When she opened her eyes, the first thing she saw was the shotgun. It startled her awake.

"That colored girl's run off," Seth said. "Don't ask me why. I was at the kitchen table figuring out those steps, and I heard the back door bang. She hightailed it into the woods."

"What's that for?" Agatha said. "That dilapidated old shotgun."

"I was thinking I ought to go out after her."

"With a gun?" Agatha set aside the sewing basket she still held in her lap. "What's Raymond going to say?"

"I don't know." It was more a question of what Raymond was going to do. "He's no brother of mine."

"He won't believe she just ran off," Agatha said. "He'll blame you."

Seth went to the sideboard and rummaged through the drawer where he had last seen the shotgun shells. Way at the back he located a box with a half-dozen dull red cartridges in it. Bird shot. The narrow yellow carton was empty, but under a rust-stained rag he found a can of light oil. He arranged the shells and the oil on the table.

"So I better be ready for him," Seth said. He sat down and opened the oil can. The cap was rusted on; when he wrenched it loose he could feel his eyeballs bulge in his head.

Agatha stood over him. "I won't have you shooting that thing," she said.

"You don't have anything to say about it," he said. "If I got to protect myself, I will."

"That shotgun belonged to my grandpa," she said.

"I know that."

"He never fired it in his whole life, and neither did my daddy. That gun's not been fired in probably forty or fifty years."

"It's whole," Seth said. "It ain't lost none of its parts, so I imagine it'll still fire when I load it and pull the trigger."

"Look how rusty it is," Agatha said. "What if it blows up in your face?"

"That's why I'm sitting here with this rag and this can of oil."

"Raymond has a strong attachment to that girl," she said.

"I had a good look at his attachment," Seth said.

"Her mother and father got killed when somebody set off a bomb. They were in a Baptist church down South. Raymond's taken care of her ever after."

Seth nudged the muzzle of the gun under Lana's white underpants and lifted them toward the ceiling. "Pow," he said. "Pow." Both barrels.

Agatha turned away.

"Suit yourself," she said.

For a long time he worked at the shotgun, while Agatha stood at the sink, peeling potatoes for supper. Gradually the brown and orange rust disappeared and the bluish color of the barrels emerged, glowing like night sky, under his hands. Seth hoped—truly—he'd have no call to shoot the gun. What if it did explode?

"It looks sound enough to me," he told Agatha, but she seemed not to hear him.

Just at dusk the rain began, with lightning and thunder, but nothing so close as last night's storm. The drops pelted the roof and the west side of the house and streamed down the windows, blurring the woods where he had last seen Lana. He thought of the colored girl wrapped in the white sheet— how she would be drenched and cold, how the wetness would freshen the look of the blood on her legs—and he wondered if she had really miscarried Raymond's baby, or if the blood was only the ordinary curse of being a woman. You couldn't believe anything those people said; you couldn't sort out the lies from the truth. He wasn't even sure he believed the story about someone bombing a church. Who would do such a thing? Animals. Monkey-people. And she'd had the nerve to tell him he was the uncivilized one. When he sat down to the supper of stew beef and boiled potatoes, the thought of Lana Windham choked him, and he was aware that Aggie watched him with genuine alarm.

"Don't bolt your food," she said.

He ate in silence. The shotgun was leaned against the wall beside the porch door. He'd loaded it, wiped the corrosion off the brass casings and forced the shells into both breech openings. He'd tucked a couple of extra shells into the pocket of his overalls.

"Make a pot of coffee," he told Agatha. "So I can stay awake tonight."

After supper he went out to his porch, to the fresh smell of the pine lumber, his heart lifted by it. Then he thought of Raymond and Lana, and his heart dropped. For a long time he sat at the end of the porch nearest the road, his legs dangling, the shotgun across his lap. The last of the storm clouds passed; in their wake they left a thin ground fog that shimmered between him and the nearby trees under the light of a swollen moon. He half-expected Lana Turner Windham to rise from the mists and come toward him, arms outstretched, eyes popped out, moaning like a ghost. Of course, that was baloney. Driven off, afraid of what he might do to her, she would sure never appear of her own free will. And she might die out there—might drown in the weed-green lake —in which case she'd never appear at all. Seth brooded on that.

But Raymond would. Raymond would be back sometime, a doctor in tow, maybe a minister tagging along for Aggie's sake; witnesses to whatever happened. He shivered. What would Raymond do? He was not a big man, but he was a crazy one—what normal man would love a colored girl and bring her to live with whites?—and crazy men had unpredictable strengths. Look what he'd done in the kitchen. It made Seth mad to think that all this mess had started because he cared about his own property, and it made him even madder that he could not tell where the mess was going to end. These woods had always hidden him from the world. Now they hid his enemies; he could not see who or what was coming, and even if he could, there was no escape because Raymond had the truck.

He sat tensely on the raw boards, turning his face toward every small noise, hitching the shotgun from one knee to the other. It might be animals he heard in the wet leaves, or an owl waking for the night's hunt, or Lana Windham lost, or Raymond blind with rage. God knew what. In the stark moonlight he made out the shadow of Agatha's orange cat, and he raised the gun, sighting at the cat, thinking what the bird shot would do to it. Not much. He wished the shells were loaded with buckshot; he had seen what buckshot could do to a living thing, how at so close a range it could tear a squirrel or a rabbit to shreds. "Pow," he whispered, imagining the cat dead in the middle of the clearing.

He would have to let Raymond come closer than that. He would be standing as Raymond stepped down from the truck

cab and came toward the porch, tracking him with the shotgun, knowing that if Raymond wanted to get at him he would
have to climb up awkwardly because the steps weren't built,
and in that clumsy instant Raymond would be at his mercy.
He would point the gun into Raymond's face; if he had to—
if it was a matter of saving himself and what was important to
his life—he would pull the triggers, one after the other.
"Pow," he said to the darkness all around him. "Pow." Both
damned barrels.

Feature Presentations

"It kills me how you can spoil a trip so consistently," Harriet said. "Every year when we come to see your father, I think it's going to be different, but it never is."

"It kills me too," Philip said. He was propped against a pair of pillows on one of the motel room's two double beds, watching television with the sound turned down. He had poured two fingers of Scotch into a plastic tumbler, which he held against his chest while he waited for the granddaughter, Rachel, to come back from the ice machine. The Scotch had been inside his suitcase in the trunk of the car; it was warm, almost hot.

"I love Maine," his wife said. "I hate to have it ruined for me."

"I don't mean to ruin it." He watched her slide the green ice chest to the edge of the bathroom sink and unscrew the petcock. Water that had been the ice from yesterday's motel burst out and gurgled down the sink drain. "Anyway, we're here."

He looked broodingly into the dark liquid in his glass. By small pressure from his hands he could squeeze the tumbler into interesting oval shapes, but he had to be careful not to crack the plastic.

"Where the devil is Rachel?" he said. "Why don't you let me have a little ice from the chest."

Harriet held out her hand. "Give me your glass."

"Thanks." He watched her draw up a fistful of ice and slide it down the inside of the tumbler, careful not to splash out any of the Scotch.

"Just let this keep draining while Rachel and I have a swim," she said. "I'll fill it up later."

"Whatever you say."

She held the drink toward him. "Enough?"

Philip nodded and took it from her. He swirled the ice around and drank. "I needed that," he said.

There was a gentle knock at the door.

"Don't you pick on that child," Harriet warned. "She's been a perfect little angel."

While his wife and granddaughter put on their bathing suits to go out to the pool, Philip turned his attention to the television. A movie was playing; the motel had HBO or Showtime or some such—it was impossible to know unless you were on hand for the beginning of a feature and could see the fancy graphics that identified the cable channel. A band of caped men on horseback was galloping across the screen, in pursuit of some goal which, given Philip's earlier inattention, was ephemeral, or magical, or merely obscure.

"Everybody and his dog was getting ice," Rachel said. "I drank a can of Pepsi while I was waiting."

"That stuff will rot your stomach lining," Philip said, not taking his eyes from the television horsemen.

"Not as bad as what you're drinking."

"She's right," Harriet said. She stood in a black one-piece suit behind Rachel, pushing wisps of hair under her bathing cap.

"No comment," Philip said. "Grandfathers are immune to criticism." He sipped his Scotch and set the glass on the bedside table. The silent horsemen had arrived at a cabin overlooking an arroyo, where they were met by a young woman wearing a long skirt and a plain shirtwaist. He wondered what they had to tell one another.

"Hurry up, honey," Harriet said. "Get into your suit and I'll race you to the pool."

At the edge of his vision Philip could see Rachel pulling the white swimsuit up her tanned legs and sliding the straps over her narrow shoulders. His granddaughter was nine; she seemed to him a perfect miniature of a strikingly attractive adult, with straight blonde hair, graceful arms and long, well-shaped legs; during the trip he had sometimes had to remind himself that she was a very young child and the daughter of his elder son. Shortly after he and Harriet agreed to take Rachel east with them, Philip had begun remembering a day in the nineteen-forties when he had been caught staring between the legs of a girl cousin—Samantha, six or seven years old, on her way to bed in a cotton undershirt. It was his Uncle Raymond, now long dead, who saw where he was looking; the man said nothing, only frowned and shook his head. Philip had felt smothered by guilt. My own cousin, he told himself that night, tossing in the guest bedroom he shared with his parents. My own cousin! He was sweaty with shame. He had been—what? Twelve? Thirteen? Now here he was, nearly sixty years old, and his uncle's disapproval still sent a hot wave of embarrassment over him.

"You ladies be careful in the water," he said.

"Please don't drink too much," Harriet said. She drew open the drapes and slid back the glass door that led onto the green poolside carpeting.

"Doesn't Grampa ever swim?" Rachel asked.

"Your grandfather is not amphibious," Harriet said. She nudged Rachel out the door.

"I'll call Aunt Pat," Philip said.

"That's a very good idea. Give her my love." She paused in the doorway. "Seriously," she said, "go easy with Johnnie Walker."

"Moderation in all things," Philip said.

For a few minutes Philip watched his wife and granddaughter cavorting in the blue pool—the little girl belly-flopping off the springboard at the deep end and splashing to the ladder in a flutter of arms and legs, the woman performing one flat, no-nonsense dive from the side of the pool and swimming with her easy crawl stroke from end to end and back.

He finished the watery Scotch in his glass and got up for a refill, taking ice cubes out of the motel's bucket and splashing liquor over them. He turned up the television volume on the way past. A classic gunfight was in progress, people clutching themselves and falling dead; he lowered the sound again. He leaned against the pillows, sipped his drink, set the tumbler aside. Harriet and Rachel were slapping green water at each other.

The local phone book was not in the drawer of the nightstand. Philip wandered around the room, opening other drawers—in the writing table before the window, in each low dresser—until he found a tattered directory and looked up his aunt's number. The phone rang six times before it was answered by a voice he managed to place as belonging to his cousin Charlotte, Aunt Pat's youngest daughter.

"The family's Midwestern branch has arrived," Philip said. He tried to put into his voice the jauntiness he did not feel. "Safely ensconced at ye olde Holiday Inn."

"You probably wonder what *I'm* doing here," Charlotte said. "Actually, I came a day early for the funeral."

"Funeral?" Philip sat up and put both feet flat on the floor between the beds. Aunt Pat was his favorite. "Whose funeral?"

"Uncle Eric's."

"I'll be damned." Aunt Pat's black-sheep brother. He sank back into the pillows and retrieved the drink with his free hand. He had not seen Uncle Eric in ten years—had seen him perhaps a half-dozen times in his whole life.

"You hadn't heard?" Charlotte said. "No, of course you hadn't, being on the road. He died day before yesterday. He'd been lingering forever, at that nursing home in Wiscasset."

"When's the service?"

"Tomorrow at two. Why? Do you want to go?"

"Not really," Philip said. "But since we're here . . ."

"That would please Aunt Christine, I know," Charlotte said. "And seeing you and Harriet would make the whole affair a lot less dreary for me."

"How's Aunt Chris taking it?"

"I'm not sure she's aware of it. What catches your attention when you're ninety-one?"

Then Aunt Pat was on the line and he could ask about his father. "How's the old man?" was what he said to her.

"I'm just giving him his supper," Aunt Pat said. "Shall I bring him to the phone?"

"No, just tell him we're in town and I'll see him in the morning," Philip said. "Do you suppose he'll want to attend the funeral? He kind of liked Eric at one time."

"Oh, I don't think so," Aunt Pat said. "He has such a hard time getting around now. I think the ride to Wiscasset, and the climbing in and out of the car, would be awfully tiring for him."

"He's okay, though?"

"Oh my, yes. You know your father. He slows down, but he doesn't stop."

"He's lucky to have you to keep an eye on him, Aunt Pat."

"Well," she said brightly, "we're company for each other."

"Just give him my love," Philip said.

* * *

Harriet stood in a half-slip between Philip and the television screen—the Western seemed eternal—holding the liquor bottle up to him.

"There can't be more than two swallows left in it," she said. "You promised moderation."

"It's my unwinding supply," Philip said. "Now that we've arrived, I can unwind for one last time, can't I?"

"What will you do for the trip home?"

He put out his lower lip. "Aren't we going to stop in New Hampshire for cheap Glenlivet?"

"You joke about pouting," Harriet said, "but you pout, in fact, all the time." She set the bottle down and resumed drying her hair with one of the pool towels. The room smelled oppressively of chlorine. Rachel had followed her grandmother into the shower; Philip listened to the water rumbling into the tub and whining in the walls.

"It's a wonderful start to a vacation," Harriet said. "I didn't bring one stitch that's appropriate for a funeral."

"I've been thinking," Philip said, "that maybe we should just skip it after all."

"You said we'd go. What will anybody think if we don't show up now?"

"Or you and Rachel could stay here and I'll go alone. It's my family; not yours."

"It's my family too," Harriet said. "I married into it, you may recall."

Philip sighed loudly and drank.

Harriet flung the wet towel at him. "Oh, shut up," she said. She stood before the mirror over the sink and ran a comb through her hair—dark brown hair shot through with so much gray that lately Philip felt a twinge of surprise whenever he really saw his wife. "If you want to do a nice thing for me someday, give me a hair dryer for traveling."

"Someday," he said. "What about dinner?"

"We could eat in the room. We've got all that sandwich stuff in the chest."

"Why don't we feed Rachel that; then you and I can have a leisurely dinner—a grown-up dinner—in the restaurant."

She studied him for a moment. "All right," she said. "Let's do that."

Philip saluted her with his drink as Rachel bounded out of the bathroom, naked, a white towel wound around her wet hair. The child stood at the foot of the bed, eyes closed, arms stretched out in front of her. She was not exactly a miniature adult, Philip noted before he looked away.

"I am the Swami," Rachel intoned. "I can read your past and your future."

Philip let his gaze rest on the television picture. "What about my present?" he asked her.

Rachel opened her eyes and let her arms fall to her sides. "You can read it for yourself," she said. "This *is* the present."

"That's what I was afraid of," Philip said.

"It must be like a sea change," Harriet said, "what happens to you. It's like the way your accent begins to come back as soon as we hit the Berkshires, only it's an alteration somewhere inside you."

Philip shrugged; he was hunched, elbows on the table, over the Rob Roy the waitress had brought him across the nearly empty restaurant. "I'm just tired," he said. "And I'm not crazy about funerals."

"You shouldn't have offered to go."

"The man shouldn't have passed on while I was in the neighborhood." He lifted the stemmed glass; the cocktail was dry and not unpleasant. "It's only three years since my mother died."

"I know."

"Anyway, this is the time of my life I've been dreading for

years—the time when that whole generation is about to be wiped out. They're all in their eighties, you know."

"I know."

"Dad's eighty-eight. Aunt Pat is eighty-three. Aunt Christine is ninety-one, for God's sake."

"I just think you could be more philosophical about it," Harriet said. "Shouldn't we order? The restaurant closes at ten."

"And Rachel." Philip opened the menu. "Children are no longer appropriate to my life. I'm never quite sure how to deal with Rachel."

"She's very self-sufficient for her age," Harriet said.

"I'll say."

"What is that supposed to mean? Rachel's been delightful company."

"She's a distraction," Philip said.

"Oh yes," Harriet said. "I see the way you look at her."

"There must be something wrong with me," Philip said.

"I doubt it. You never had a daughter, and Rachel is a pretty little girl. Of course she turns your head. And she's bright."

"Precocious," Philip said.

"No, she's probably typical of nine-year-olds nowadays. But she's just not like the nine-year-olds you and I used to know."

"It's scary."

"Just don't imagine she's flirting with you," Harriet said. "Give her four or five more years for that, after she's got through being a fat little twelve-year-old, and turned into a sexy teen-ager. By which time you may be too old for incest."

"Spare me," Philip said.

"Are you really going to brood for the rest of the trip about sex and death?"

"Certainly," he said. "Isn't that what men do when they visit their fathers?"

* * *

Next morning, standing under the extraordinary force of the motel shower, Philip rehearsed meeting his father. The encounter would be filled, as it always was, with disjunctions, striking silences, as if neither man could sustain adult conversation.

"How's everything going?" he would ask.

"I'm as well as can be expected," his father would say. "My eyes keep getting worse."

The television set in Aunt Pat's front room would be on, a game show or a sports event blaring from the screen, his father's feet resting on the needlepoint footstool in front of his easy chair.

"I've got a little T.V. up in my room, on the bureau, but it's not connected to the cable," his father would say. "I watch for a while after I get into bed. Patricia turns off the set when she comes upstairs."

"That's real service." Philip would be conscious of shouting against the deafness which had become one more barrier separating him from the old man. Then a silence, the two of them sitting as if tongue-tied, watching whatever was on the tube.

"The Red Sox are having tough sledding the last week or so," Philip would say.

"They can't stand prosperity." His father would fold his hands across his stomach, lean his head back against the antimacassar. "They had a three to nothing lead last night; lost the game four to three in the tenth. They have a dickens of a time with Detroit." Philip would think: how thin he is, how frail. "I wanted to tell you"—his father had said this the last time they were together—"that I want a military funeral. You'll have to get in touch with the American Legion commander; I think his name is Johnson, or Jameson."

"It'll be a long time before we have to worry about that." Shouted.

"Just don't forget. A military funeral."

"But it's crazy," Philip said to Harriet. He stood at the

sink, a towel wrapped around him, shaving for the first time
in three days. "He was only in the army for six months in
1918. He never got nearer the war than Officer Candidate
School at Plattsburgh."

"It won't hurt you to humor him," Harriet said.

"I know." He rinsed his face and dried it. "Where's
Rachel?"

"I sent her to read, out by the pool."

"Is she all set to go?"

"Yes." Harriet surveyed him. "Are you?"

"I will be." He rummaged through his suitcase after underwear and socks. "We have to find a laundromat," he said.

"Across the street from your old high school," Harriet said.
"The one where everybody sweats." She sidled past him to
pick up the ice bucket. "I'm going to fill up the ice chest. I
don't want to lose that nice liverwurst we bought in Bridge-
port."

"Take the key."

Philip finished dressing. When Harriet came back with the
ice he had put on a necktie and was just slipping into his navy
blazer.

"That's a smashing outfit," Harriet said. "Just the thing for
mourning."

"Listen," he said, "did you tell Rachel she'd be staying
home? I think Charlotte's youngest boy is just a couple of
years older. They can entertain each other."

"You tell her," Harriet said. "I know she's counting on
going. She told me she's never seen a dead man before."

Aunt Pat's house on Spring Street was a faded blue saltbox
with bay windows and a long side porch. It was in far better
shape than he'd remembered it, the enormous chimneys at
either end of the roof looking to have been recently tuck-
pointed, and the roof itself newly shingled. Upstairs on the
right were the windows of the room where his mother had

died, and her mother before her. Now it was his father's room.

"It only needs a little paint," Harriet said. "It's a gorgeous old house."

"How old?" Rachel asked.

"We don't know, honey," Harriet said. "Probably at least two hundred years."

"Wow," Rachel said. "Can I use the door-knocker?" She stood on her tiptoes to use the brass knocker.

Philip watched the muscles tighten in the backs of her legs. "Cousin Charlotte has a boy just about your age," he said. "I think his name is Richard."

"Richards are know-it-alls," Rachel said. "Richard Dunstan, Richard Morrell, Richard Drury."

"Who are those people?"

"Three Richards in the fourth grade."

Charlotte opened the door to them. "Sorry for the slowness," she said. "Up to my elbows, giving Mother her bath."

In the dark front hall the two women hugged; Philip gave Charlotte a peck on the cheek. Behind her, a small boy wearing glasses stood on one foot in the doorway between the hall and the front room.

"This is our granddaughter, Rachel—Timmy's girl."

Rachel put out her hand; Charlotte pressed it between both of hers. "I'm happy to meet you, Rachel," she said. "How old are you?"

"I'm nine."

"Then you must meet Richard." She motioned to the boy. "He's just turned eleven."

"Hello," Rachel said to him. "I hear you're very smart."

Richard came into the hall, carrying what appeared to be a model airplane. He looked mortified—whether from Rachel's sarcasm or the prospect of having to baby-sit the girl, Philip couldn't tell. "Do you want to come upstairs and see my projects?" Richard asked.

"Is that the *Enterprise?*" Rachel said. She followed him up the stairs. "Are you some kind of Trekkie?"

"What do you hear from your sister Samantha?" Philip said. "She still in Italy?"

"She was home in May for Harold's wedding." Charlotte led them into the den. "Here she is with the bride and groom."

Photographs in small gold-colored frames were on every surface—on the mantel over the fireplace, on top of the old upright piano, on the drum table under the window. Philip had long ago given up trying to keep track of the faces displayed; they were children and grandchildren of girl cousins he had not seen in a score of years.

"Hard to believe Sam's got children old enough to be married," Philip said. He put on his glasses to look at the wedding snapshot. Samantha beamed beside her tall son; late forties, was she? Fifties? How was that possible?

"Here's Mother." Charlotte met Aunt Pat in the doorway and put an arm around her shoulders.

"Aunt Pat." Philip bent to kiss the woman. Over the years, she had grown smaller and rounder. Her hair was cut short, and her face had gotten puffy and florid. When he was a boy, he had liked her perfume, and once he crept into the bedroom she shared with Uncle Raymond to discover the ink-blue "Evening in Paris" bottle. Today Aunt Pat smelled of Ivory soap. "The world changes," he said, "but you don't."

"What a nice liar," Aunt Pat said. She turned to kiss Harriet. "Make him tell the truth at least once a week."

"He's getting better at it," Harriet said.

"I see you're admiring my rogues' gallery." Aunt Pat stood before the mantelpiece and put out one hand to steady herself. "I have thirteen grandchildren and four great-grandchildren."

"And counting," Charlotte said.

"Charlie," Aunt Pat said, "I think we should sit in the front room. And I think perhaps I'll take one of those pills." She paused in the doorway. "Your father," she said to Philip. "I think he expects you to come up to his room."

* * *

Philip's father was apologetic. "Usually I come downstairs for breakfast," he said. "Then I watch my game shows. They've been replaying the last Olympics on one of those sports channels; I enjoy that too." He pawed at a checkered afghan thrown over the arm of his chair.

"Do you want me to put that across your legs?"

His father hesitated. "Not now," he said.

"Harriet's downstairs with Aunt Pat and Charlotte," Philip said in a loud voice. "She'll be up in a few minutes."

"Who?"

"Harriet."

"Is she with you?"

"Yes. She's down talking with Aunt Pat."

His father nodded. "I thought I'd stay put today," he said. "But I don't have cable up here."

"How's everything going?" Philip said. "How do you feel?"

"My eyes keep getting worse. Charlotte drove me to Portland last month to see a specialist. He said there wasn't anything he could do at my age—that if I were younger . . ." His voice trailed off, and he folded his hands across his stomach. "Thirty dollars," he said, "just to tell me that."

"Do you want to go with us to Eric's funeral?" Philip said.

His father's face went blank. "Who?" he said.

"Eric. Aunt Pat's brother."

"Is Eric dead?"

"Three days ago."

His father shook his head sadly. "I want a military funeral," he said. "You won't forget?"

"I won't forget," Philip said.

"You've got the key to my safe-deposit box?"

"Yes, I've still got it."

His father looked out the window. Philip sat on the edge of the bed, waiting. He racked his brain for something to say.

"Our granddaughter is here with us," he said. "Rachel. Tim's little girl."

"Tim?" his father said.

Philip leaned closer. "Listen," he said. "I'll be right back. I'm going downstairs to get Harriet to say hello to you."

Uncle Eric's services were held at a red-brick funeral home whose rooms were decorated with brocade draperies and mottled, wine-dark carpeting. The people attending, Philip thought, were not so much mourners as guests at a reunion: so much chatter, so much embracing and smiling and handshaking. He felt entirely out of place, a stranger among relatives who had never met him and so could not acknowledge his relationship.

Harriet leaned to whisper: "Do you see anyone else you know?"

"Not a soul."

They sat at the back of a dingy room filled with an assortment of folding chairs and settees, Harriet trim in a cream-colored summer suit, Philip too warm in his blazer over gray slacks, Rachel in a pale-blue frock that matched the ribbon in her hair. Throughout the eulogy, Philip was aware at the edge of his vision of Rachel's white ankle socks and black-patent shoes dancing endlessly. The movement distracted him from the musty air of the parlor.

"He still wants the military funeral," he whispered. "And this time he asked me if I had his safe-deposit key."

"Well, you do."

"Certainly, I do—except don't you remember? I opened the box two years ago when he had the bypass. There's nothing in it except his army discharge and the transcript of his freshman grades at Amherst."

Harriet sighed. "Just humor him," she said.

Afterward, they congregated with Aunt Pat and Charlotte and Charlotte's Richard outside the funeral home.

"Uncle Eric never looked so neat in his life," Philip said. "Whatever's the male equivalent of a bag lady—that was Eric."

"I liked him," Rachel said. "He looked like an old-man doll, just exactly."

"Way too much rouge," Harriet said.

"Poor Eric," Aunt Pat said. "He was such a smart boy—so creative. He'd have been the star of the family if his luck hadn't been so bad."

"What did he do?" Rachel asked. "How was he creative?"

"He was an inventor," Philip said.

"What did he invent?"

"What a shame Christine couldn't come," said Aunt Pat. "I haven't seen her in years and years." She squeezed Philip's arm, the pressure of her fingers sharp but not suggesting strength. "Your father," she said. "How he perks up when you come to visit!"

"I'm glad we did our duty," Harriet said, "but I must say I was relieved we didn't follow to the cemetery."

"Nobody ever did tell me what Uncle Eric invented," Rachel said. She was sitting cross-ankled on her bed, a book in her lap, a can of Pepsi in one hand.

"The truth is, I don't think anybody knows," Philip said. "He just spent all his time at garage sales and flea markets, buying up junk."

"You never saw anything he built?"

"Never. Anyway, I didn't see Uncle Eric and Aunt Chris very often. But once I saw Eric's kidney stones."

"For heaven's sake," Harriet said.

"It's true. Aunt Chris kept them in a jam jar on the mantelpiece, pickled in alcohol." He sat on the bed. "I just remembered that," he said. "I haven't thought of it in years."

"If cousin Charlotte is your cousin," Rachel said, "is silly Richard my cousin?"

"I don't know," Philip said. "I've never been able to figure that one out. Richard is either your first cousin, twice removed, or your second cousin, once removed. Or he's neither one. Relatives are very complicated."

"Is Aunt Pat my aunt?"

"She's your great-great-aunt," Harriet said.

"Richard says she's dying," Rachel said. She took a swallow of Pepsi. "He says little pieces of Aunt Pat's bones are breaking off all the time, and that's why she sits so much—so the bones won't break any faster. He says Aunt Pat has to take lots of pills for pain, and that makes her spacey. That's why Cousin Charlotte moved in with her, to take care of her and Great-Grampa."

Philip looked at Harriet, who stopped folding the blouse she had worn to the funeral. "My God," he said.

"That explains some things," Harriet said. She put the blouse up to her face, then laid it on top of her suitcase.

"I thought you guys knew all that," Rachel said.

"No," Philip said. "We just thought Aunt Pat was getting older, like we all are." In his mind's eye, Aunt Pat stood before him with her five small daughters; he imagined her just thirty, jolly over the cooking, the laundry, the ironing. The caring. "Such loving energy," his mother used to say. In his mind Aunt Pat was saying, "Lucky Philip. You have five cousins, but they have only you."

"Is it some kind of cancer?" Harriet said.

Rachel tipped the book up and leaned her chin against it. "Should I not have told?" she said.

That night, while Rachel got ready for bed, the two grandparents sat in a silence Philip supposed was laden with the freight of the day's mortality. Harriet sat at the round writing table and worried at her nails, buffing and filing, the drop lamp shading the side of her face nearest Philip. Philip lay across the rumpled bed that had become his refuge from the letdown of the trip and the depressing encounters of the arrival. He had found the television movie schedule, bound in its imitation-leather cover like a wine list, fallen behind the set, and now he was studying it.

"It's Showtime, by the way," he said.

"I know." Harriet did not look up from her nails.

"How did you know?"

"That Western you were watching yesterday. We saw it in Ann Arbor. I don't remember the name of the movie, but it was Showtime."

Philip put the schedule aside and watched Rachel at the sink, brushing her teeth—tiny, even teeth, so white and regular they might have belonged to a film star. How coolly she had delivered the lines about Aunt Pat's sickness. Such absence of self-consciousness. Suppose the Angel of Death turned out to be a blonde child with a perfect bite.

"Don't forget to floss," he told the girl, "or else your teeth will fall out like your grandfather's."

Rachel half-turned and grinned at him over her shoulder. "You've got teeth," she said. "Like the Big Bad Wolf's."

Philip looked guiltily at Harriet. "I didn't know kids still read those old-fashioned stories," he said.

"It's a classic," Rachel said. She bared her teeth and leaned toward the mirror to study them. "Like 'Mirror, mirror on the wall.' "

"Hurry along, honey," Harriet said. "It's way past ten-thirty."

"I'm ready." Rachel switched off the lights above the mirror and whirled into the center of the room. Her short, flowered nightgown had matching panties, and she still wore the pale-blue ribbon in her hair. She was cradling a panda bear, which seemed to be her constant bed partner; in Cheektowaga, when Philip at first forgot to bring the panda in from the car, a scene—the only one of the four-day drive—had ensued.

"Give us a kiss good-night," Philip said.

He held out his arms. Rachel slid between them and gave him a toothpaste-scented kiss on the cheek. " 'Night, Grampa," she said. "Sleep tight."

"You too, sweetie." It charmed him to think that his next

day would begin with this pretty creature climbing onto the bed with them—to think of her suppleness, her sleep-warmth, her morning breath like the subtle perfume of wild-flowers. It was true, what he had said to Harriet at dinner yesterday, that children were no longer appropriate to his life. But I'm all right, he told himself; I just have to relearn them, their ways of affection. It was with sincere reluctance that he let her go to Harriet.

" 'Night, Gram."

"Good-night, honey. Pleasant dreams."

After Harriet arranged the covers, and Rachel had gotten the panda bear's small head comfortably settled on the pillow beside her, Philip turned out the lights between the beds. He watched the child until he was sure she was asleep, before he went to fetch ice cubes and make himself a drink from the last of the Scotch.

Harriet, who was already in bed, seemed surprised. "I should think you'd be wiped out," she said.

"I am," he said. "What I really need to pick me up is the movie that comes on at eleven forty-five." He read from the program schedule: " 'Sexual situations, nudity, adult lan-guage.' " He rattled the ice in the plastic tumbler. "R-rated," he said. "Too bad it's not X."

Harriet turned her back to him and hugged her pillow. "You ought to be ashamed of yourself."

"Sex and death," Philip said. He took a long drink and leaned back to wait for the movie. Once, he got up to adjust the volume downward so his women would not be disturbed, and then he was surprised and amused to discover that Rachel was snoring—a soft, fluttery imitation of Harriet beside him.

He stayed awake with difficulty. Just before the film com-menced at last, an extravagant title sequence appeared, the logo of the cable channel revolving out of an infinite dis-tance, celestial images bursting across the screen to coalesce into the words FEATURE PRESENTATION. For a terrible startled instant Philip imagined the words read FUTURE GENERATIONS.

I must be getting tipsy, he thought. He started to giggle, discovered he could not stop, and when Harriet propped herself on one elbow to ask what was the matter, for heaven's sake, he realized how helpless he was to answer.

Braid

We're on our way to lunch—a cold October rain is falling in Charleston, so Carla has suggested to Weymouth that we drive to the restaurant—and we have just turned the corner of Lee onto Quarrier when we see the girl with the long hair. She is tall and slender, with trim ankles; she wears a black dress printed with pink flowers and carries a pink umbrella. Her hair is honey-blonde, woven into a single braid, and the braid flows down her back to her calves. The length is extraordinary; the end of the braid—the last five or six inches aren't plaited—follows her across the street like a tail.

"Look at that," Weymouth says.

"Imagine taking care of it," Carla says from the back seat.

By now we have passed the girl. I turn to see her face, but she has vanished. "You ought to let yours grow that long," I say to Carla.

"It wouldn't get to that length. I can't even grow it long enough to sit on."

I face front and watch the wipers sweep the windshield. I used to be in love with Carla, in a manner of speaking. Twenty years ago at a college in Vermont I was her piano instructor, though not her first. Clive Blair was the first.

"Think how much that hair must weigh," Weymouth says.

"And even more if the rain gets it wet," I say. "Imagine washing it."

"I wonder how she brushes it," Carla says. "Though I suppose she just brings it all forward, over one shoulder." She leans between us; her longish hair, just for an instant, touches my cheek. "You can see why she keeps it braided."

"Lady Godiva must have had hair that long," I say.

Weymouth says, "We had an Angora cat named Godiva. Every summer she wandered through the cockleburs until we couldn't pull them out of her. We used to have to shave her belly."

"I don't know about the Lady," Carla says, "but when my mother was a girl, her hair was almost to her knees."

"Godiva the cat was so embarrassed," Weymouth says, "she hid under the front porch until her fur grew back."

"Poor creature," Carla says.

Yesterday Carla stayed home from the office, and when I came downstairs she was in the kitchen, loading the dishwasher. I'd lain awake a long time, almost since daybreak. The crowing of a rooster somewhere close by had occupied me a while. I was slow to realize what it was, and when I did, the cliché surprised me. Bucolic. Rustic. Uncommon words since I moved to Boston. I turned over and drew the pillow under my cheek and watched the morning light spill slowly through the east-facing windows—no sun because the mountain would block it until ten o'clock or so—and listened to the rooster advertise himself. The last geranium blooms reddened in the window boxes; the trees kept most of their leaves, though by now they were rust and gold and yellow; some sort of ivy that fringed the windows was already bare.

I don't know what I thought would happen if I stayed in bed. I heard the school bus stop for Carla's daughter, Kate. I heard Weymouth drive away in the Blazer—saw him, actually, framed for a moment or two in one of the bedroom windows before the truck disappeared around the right-hand curve that sloped up the steep ridge where he would have to shift into four-wheel drive.

I suppose I hoped Carla would come into the room to wake me, that she would sit on the edge of the bed and push the hair back from my brow—mother-like—and that perhaps she would kiss me, my eyes, my mouth, whispering, "What do you want for breakfast?" You, I would answer. Just as I had wanted her after poor Clive died and I watched her haunted face in class and in the halls of the music building.

Finally I obliged myself to rise and dress, to carry out the duties of every morning and leave my imagination alone. I sat at the table in the country kitchen, my vitamin pills laid out before me on the cloth, and watched Carla. Coffee she brought me, and tomato juice to wash down my pills. Her eyes still held a sadness—a melancholy, I suppose, that had nothing to do with weighty matters, but simply with the everyday conditions of life. Clive had doted on her. Carla this, Carla that. Her talent, her beauty, even the reach of her fingers on the keyboard. He talked about her whenever we were together. Once, in the departmental coffee room, he was overheard by old Klaus Grunwald, who taught the brasses.

"It is not proper to talk so of one's pupils," Grunwald told him. "And in any case, you cannot tell if a woman is beautiful until at least she is in her thirties."

Now Carla is thirty-nine. Grunwald was right, and so was Clive.

Weymouth Shaw is a lawyer and Carla is a social worker. It is a partnership that goes back to the years of conscience and

high purpose that began with J.F.K. and flowered in the late
nineteen-sixties and early -seventies, when the two of them
were VISTA volunteers in Appalachia. Now Weymouth is in
environmental law—knowledgeable about job compensation
and corporate abuses of the West Virginia landscape. Carla
has become intimate with the deprivation of these hills and
hollows, and is a genius of the heart's geography.

"The world savages these people," Carla says at lunch.
"Even if they own the land, it's theirs only on the surface.
The mineral rights, the natural-gas deposits—some faceless
man in New York or Chicago or Dallas owns them and gets
rich off them. It's rotten."

"But legal," Weymouth says.

Carla looks at me helplessly. "Why I couldn't be a lawyer,"
she says. "That scrupulous avoidance of compassion."

Weymouth shakes his head and takes a gulp of red wine.
"Carla has no patience with reality. I keep telling her it's
case-by-case, that you can't reform the world with some kind
of moralistic magic wand."

"I understand cases," she says. "So get off mine."

"I had a fellow in the office this morning," Weymouth tells
me, "just before you two came to meet me. Black lung—"

"Jesus," Carla says. "Another one."

"Always," Weymouth says. "Man about fifty, fifty-five, but
looking seventy." He stops. "They look starved—their faces
—and ravaged, all of them, and they have that ugly cough."

"It's criminal," Carla says.

"And yet they're vital men. I mean it: vital. Good-hu-
mored. A grasp of irony—they know the coal companies have
screwed them over, but hell, it's a living. That marvelous
respect for authority—they practically bow to me when they
come into the office. It isn't as if they felt inferior to me, but
they sense the distinction between a profession and a job."

"Oh, stop it," Carla says.

"What?" Weymouth says. "Stop what?"

"This goddamned condescension of yours."

Weymouth's shoulders slump and he dabs at his mouth with the napkin. "Pardon me all to hell," he says. Then he straightens up and gives me a wry look. "That's Carla's egalitarian pose," he says. "But if it was an artist—a musician, let's say—who came into my office with his hat in his hands, that would be another story. I'd be allowed to distinguish him from the common herd, wouldn't I, babe?"

I watch the color fade from Carla's cheeks and the restaurant lights flare in her brown eyes.

"If looks could kill," says her husband. He puts a forefinger to his temple and cocks his thumb.

When lunch is over, we drive to the train station. Weymouth has a conference in Washington; he is one of three lawyers preparing to argue a case before the Supreme Court. "One of the big chemical companies. They're absolutely murdering nature around here."

"Poison," Carla says, after she has kissed Weymouth goodbye outside the station. "That's all the companies know. Poison the workers, poison the air and water, poison the soul."

"How do they poison the soul?"

She shifts the Blazer into first gear, and we jolt into traffic. "Ask us to swallow their lies," she says.

We drive home in silence, Carla's attention strictly on the interstate traffic north of Charleston, her mouth set in a hard line. Once she is off I-77 she drives too fast for the narrow state road, which looks slick and menacing before us—"at Carla speed," the thirteen-year-old daughter would remind me: "There's speed, which is normal, and Carla speed, which is awesome." The truck leans hard into the curves and blunders out of them. We race past small, run-down houses and weathered shacks and barns tottering into the arms of gravity. The rain turns everything gray. Outside one shack is a tall wooden frame that displays chromed hubcaps and wheel covers, scores of them, scavenged from the ditches where the cars they decorated flung them.

*   *   *

The next day is Saturday. The morning is blue-skied, autumn-crisp, and by noon, when the sun fills the hollow, the world is warm, almost balmy. If I had not been sent to Charleston to recruit a young cellist, I would be in Boston now, looking out my studio window on a blank sky, perhaps a premonition of snow.

"We won't have many more such days," Carla says. "I think we ought to have lunch on the deck."

So we do. We sit in the sun, which by now is almost hot, and balance sandwiches on the flat arms of the deck chairs; dead leaves flutter around us, falling like petals from a gold flower. There is wine—a green bottle of a local white, something one would not have expected in West Virginia—pale and dry on the palate, perfect with the dark rye bread and the sharp cheese and the moist, pink beef. A cat, a calico with shrewd slits of eyes, who appears between us by climbing the trunk of the tree that overhangs the deck, begs beside me.

"She's ungracious," Carla says. "She'll take what you offer, and give nothing in return."

But the cat, after eating the scrap of beef I put down, nuzzles my hand and rubs against my ankles. Carla and I touch glasses.

"I think often of Clive," Carla says. She sets the glass on the deck beside her, brushes a leaf from her lap. "Times we talked. Opportunities I missed."

"Opportunities?"

"There was a vigil, something anti-war. I think four hundred of us camped on the prexy's lawn to show our opposition to the whole Vietnam mess. Clive stayed with us—a gang of us from the music department—until one or two in the morning. Then he got up to leave, making those noises he used to make about being old and not so pliant as the rest of us. 'Pliant.' I never see the word without thinking of the way he said it. 'Less pliant in my dotage,' he would say."

"I recall."

"Anyway, he paused to talk to me. 'See you later on,' he said. And then he was gone." She raises the wineglass, sips at it. "I was so young, so—so dense. I didn't realize it was a proposition until my lesson, two or three days after. He told me he'd stayed up all night, reading, waiting for me."

I nod wisely. "So it wasn't until afterward that you were lovers."

She sets the glass on the deck. When she faces me, her head tipped a little to one side as if to measure me, I see I've been wrong all these years. But she isn't angry.

"Everyone believed it," she says. "That we were lovers. I knew after the vigil that he wanted me, and God knows I'd wanted him from my first lesson with him. But it never happened."

She looks away from me. A few feet from the edge of the deck is a line of poplars, and beyond the poplars is an abandoned greenhouse, many of its small panes of glass broken out, the rest of them opaque with whitewash. The poplar leaves are yellow and tremble in the light breeze; their noise is like thin-paper pages turning. At the base of one of the trees I watch the skittish calico stretch upward to sharpen its claws.

"Then there was the wedding," Carla says, "that you were best man at. I liked Clive's new wife—Marilyn—but of course I envied her. For a long time I wouldn't come to terms with the fact of her. By the time I figured out how much I was in love with Clive, and that nothing ought to get in the way of love . . ." She stops, looks at me with a small, hopeless smile. "God, by then he was dead."

I say nothing. I remember a Monday morning in late winter, very early: the telephone call from the dean of the college. "I'm sorry to tell you this, though I don't think you'll be surprised. Clive Blair's killed himself."

Carla collects my empty plate and the green bottle. "More wine?" she asks.

I shake my head.

"I thought it would be nice to go for a walk before I have to meet Wey's train. I'll show you where we plan to build the new house."

We walk down the leaf-matted driveway, past the gray Blazer, past the blue Toyota station wagon that belongs to Carla, and we keep to the center of the road, avoiding the puddles of brown water left by yesterday's rain. To our right are thickets that become woods as the land slopes upward; to our left, on the level, are outbuildings, a stable, a broad field that includes Carla's garden.

"Potatoes," she says. "If there's time when we get back, I'll leave you for a while and do some digging."

The road where it climbs out of the hollow turns steep, and I can understand the need for four-wheel drive. It is all orange dirt, laced with white stones loosened by the recent rains. Deep channels show where the water flowed downhill in the depressions left by tire tracks, the dirt flattened and sandy as at the bottom of a dry stream bed. In the shade of overhanging maples, the dirt is still wet—mud, thick and oozy as dung. Alongside the road at intervals are low plants with vivid red leaves. Carla tells me they are sumac.

At the end of the long upward grade we arrive at a fork in the road, the right fork leading into a pale green meadow where the sun is bright and the vehicle tracks are dried yellow. There is a moment when the two of us walk from cold shadow into warm light—like passing from one room to another in an old house selectively heated.

"This way," Carla says.

It is difficult for us to walk side by side. The grade is gentler, but the ruts are deep and wide; Carla takes the grassy crown, while I keep to the shoulder. We talk across a rivulet of dun-colored sand that is punctuated with the deep hoofprints of deer.

"We've hired an architect," she says. "We brought him out here about a month ago. I'll show you the site he thought was best."

She leaves the road and strikes out through the brush into a thicket of saplings and spreading junipers. We arrive at a ridge; Carla points downward, and I see that we are overlooking the place where she and Weymouth live now: the house and deck, the dilapidated greenhouse, the garden, Weymouth and Carla's one horse—a chestnut mare that crops at the dying pasture grass so calmly, it might be the last creature on earth.

"What do you think?"

"You'll be on top of the world." I look around. Across the dirt road, the land becomes a fenced-in meadow—a hayfield, perhaps, with tall grasses gone to seed. In the meadow's center is a piece of farm machinery, abandoned, rusted so badly I can't tell what it is. At the far end of the meadow is a square of cement, railed off against casual trespass—a natural-gas well, its pipes painted bluer than the autumn sky. On the horizon, a row of steel towers supports the strands of power lines. Weymouth and Carla's house will be visible for miles.

"Good for television reception," she says. "No more frustration at Super Bowl time."

Carla paces off the dimensions of the new house, points out the kitchen, the living room, the freestanding fireplace. Here are the bedrooms; here is the solar-heated nursery for plants she will have ready to be planted outside when spring comes. Here is Weymouth's study; here is her own. They will build steps out of logs and packed dirt, leading down to the stable and a henhouse now used to store hay.

I make noises of approval. Carla is older, but not old. Her face is solemn and lovely, her eyes large, the shadows beneath them suggesting that she is tired, but she has said no, it is only her allergies that make her look so. Her mouth is full and patient. I remember that when she was a student it was her hair, falling nearly to the small of her back, that attracted me; and then her talent, and finally the serious demeanor that made her seem more reliable than other students. One day we drove together to Lake Champlain, in a sports car I used to own. We parked by the water, not far from a ferry slip, and we sat a long time in silence. What we had in common was

Clive Blair. I had been his closest friend; she had been—I believed—his lover. We held hands then and, once only, kissed. Her breath was sweet as summer. I heard no magical music, but I envied Clive—dead or not—and drove the long distance home with reluctance and satisfying guilt.

We make our way back to the narrow road, leaves and twigs crackling underfoot. Carla is ahead of me, and waits while I pluck sticktights that have caught at my socks.

"The gossip," I say, "was that the night before Clive died, his wife found him in bed with a coed, one of his pupils."

"I heard that," she says. "I even heard that it was me, but it wasn't."

"So much for gossip."

"No," Carla says. "It's never entirely dismissed, never squelched. She wrote to me—Marilyn—a couple of years after. She said she forgave me."

"And you said . . .?"

"Nothing. I wanted to tell her to go to hell, but I never answered her letter." She scuffs at a stone in the road. "We'd better start back," she says. "The potatoes have their eyes on me. And I can't be late to meet Wey's train, and Kate has to be picked up from her friends' house, and on and on and on."

"I'll look for a football game on TV," I say.

She smiles at me. "Culture," she says. "I've always thought of you as cultured."

Over our heads a bird is circling—something eagle-like that soars on the thermals and never once, in all the time I watch it, moves its wings. The undersides of those wings are shaded with narrow triangles of gray that contrast with similar shapes of white. Carla says it is a turkey vulture, and it is not so lovely as it seems.

The television room is a small, square space cluttered with magazines and sewing materials, furnished with a sofa and a pair of upholstered side chairs that have known better days.

Through the one narrow window, I can see Carla in the potato field; a wheelbarrow stands near her, and she bows to the earth with a spade, turning over the soil, kneeling to throw potatoes into the barrow. Her hair blows across her mouth, and she lifts her head to let the light wind brush it out of the way.

Carla's piano is here: a spinet, not new, with a mahogany finish much scratched—probably because it has been moved in and out of several houses since Carla's marriage. On top of it is an assortment of faded yellow Schirmer editions: Duvernoy, Schmitt, Berens, Kullak—exercise books that carry in the upper right corner of the covers Carla's graceful signature. Under the Schirmer, a thin volume of Satie divertissements. On the bottom of the stack, lesson books—Thompson, Schaum—that must be Kate's.

The piano is in tune; I play a few scales, some octaves, a pretentious chord or two. Not a hopeless instrument, but compared to the grands of a school or conservatory its music is all reticence, all suggestion too subdued to be taken to heart. STERLING, says its marque; the gold leaf of the name is blistered and starting to peel.

I stand and open the bench. Here are more piles of music, most of it dog-eared, much of it yellowed with time. I paw through it, looking for something that suits me—Schumann, perhaps, or Rachmaninoff, or Grieg.

In the bottom of the bench is a plum-colored Prokofieff sonata, the Seventh, in the Leeds Music Am-Rus edition. I slide it out into the light. It was one of Clive's favorites, though he never performed it in public—I suppose because his idol, Horowitz, played it so well and with an energy Clive feared to aspire to. He rehearsed it often in one of the college practice rooms, the lyrical second movement singing like a carillon across the campus lawns, the brilliant third swelling and crashing, fierce as waves that threatened to drown us all in passion. He was a superb performer himself.

"Why not do the Seventh at your recital?" I would say, year after year.

"Ah," he said, looking gloomy. "Too good for me; far, far too good."

Clive Blair. With Clive, you could never distinguish what he said from the pathology of his saying it. He was a prodigy whose prodigiousness had overwhelmed him at an early age. It was no secret that he had come to us straight from a psychiatric hospital, and it was no surprise that twice in the five years of his tenure with the department he took extended "vacations" at the same hospital.

"I'm a tender flower, Walter," he said to me, early on. "Too much light and I wither, too much dark and I die."

We were good friends from the beginning—we suited each other, I think, by being so unlike—and I became his confidant. When he returned to us from his vacations, he sat in the parlor of the house I rented near the college and played on an old Baldwin the pieces he had composed to amuse his fellow patients. They were intricate and small, like watches, or like the shunts and gates and pathways you would see in record-magazine photographs of a microchip. If I said I enjoyed the compositions but didn't understand them, Clive would laugh and ask what I expected from a madman.

When he talked about Carla, he was not so self-effacing. Her he took seriously. I thought he seemed genuinely in love with her, and yet was so enmeshed in the appearances of propriety and sanity that he could not bring himself to give way entirely to his emotions.

"She's too innocent to be wary of me," he said. "She doesn't see how I taint her."

That same evening, sitting in the kitchen of his apartment with a bottle of Jim Beam between us, he told me how once he had intended to hang himself—"I was standing on that chair, the chair you're sitting in, with the lamp cord around my neck"—when there was a knock on the hall door, and it was Carla.

"She saved my life," Clive said. His voice expressed awe and regret at the same time—as if Carla had been the messenger delivering a reprieve to the wrong address.

"But why did you go to the door?" I said.
I thought he knew what I meant.

The three of us spend Saturday evening quietly. Kate has
gone to bed, tired out from a day of horseback riding with her
friends. I'm reading a book of stories that I've promised to
send to Carla when I've finished. Carla is reading too, sitting
in a soft chair to the right of the fireplace with a lavender
quilt pulled up around her shoulders and across her lap, looking like some nesting creature.

Weymouth is full of himself and the preparation of his
Supreme Court brief. He has been affectionate to his wife, sly
and ironic with his daughter. To me he says, "What about a
little corn liquor?" and when I say I've never tasted it, he is
delighted.

"Now don't get carried away," Carla says.

Weymouth leads me to the kitchen, to a cupboard under
the telephone, and draws out a bourbon bottle whose label
has been obliterated with indelible ink. The liquor inside it is
clear and barely golden.

"Just a little," Weymouth says. He pours a quarter-inch
into each of two Old-Fashioned glasses and slides one toward
me. The corn liquor is smooth but strong; it leaves my throat
hot, and even the taste in my mouth is of heat, not alcohol.

"I've never had anything like it," I say.

"Makes your eyes water, doesn't it?"

"But it isn't harsh. I expected it to be harsh."

"It's all in the aging," Weymouth says. "Old Harley—he
lives in that mobile home up on the ridge—he's a past master
at moonshine. An artist."

"Wey admires artistry in all its forms," Carla says. "Artistry
and respect for authority."

Weymouth sets his jaw. "You better believe it."

"What do you suppose this is?" I say. "About a hundred-
fifty proof?"

"I wouldn't want to know." He sets the bottle on its shelf and brings out a fifth of Jack Daniel's. "Now for something a little more mundane," he says. He pours an inch of whiskey into each of the glasses, and fetches ice for us.

I'm not much of a drinker anymore. Since Clive's death, there are fewer occasions, fewer excuses. Yet tonight seems special—the three of us, Weymouth and I with our bourbon and Carla with a tiny glass of Kahlúa, settled and mellow in front of a fire to take the chill off. None of us has much to say. Weymouth has been going through the mail, and now he is reading today's *Gazette*. He is sprawled comfortably on the chaise; a white-shaded floor lamp bathes his face and his paper. Under his legs are other papers, catalogs—Heathkit, Edmund Scientific, L. L. Bean—and one tabloid, *The American Lawyer*.

"I saw Ed Lanigan today," he says, abruptly, apropos of nothing. "He was jaywalking across the Morris-Virginia intersection. Nose in a sheaf of papers."

"Pray for a truck, did you?" Carla doesn't look up from her book, but her mouth is contemptuous of Ed Lanigan. "Ed's no great favorite of this household," she says. "He's running for attorney general, with the blessing—and the money—of the mining interests."

"I think he's dyeing his hair," Weymouth says.

Carla looks over at me and raises an eyebrow in amusement. I think of yesterday, having lunch on the deck, stroking the calico cat. And what Carla said about the letter from Clive's wife. What was supposed to be forgiven? Loving, yet not loving enough?

After a while Weymouth dozes, Carla and I read, the cat strolls in and stops near the hearth to groom itself. We are like a family, I imagine, and what I feel then is an impossible mix of pleasure and sadness: that it is wonderful after twenty years to be so comfortable with Carla and with her husband; that it is a shame the one person who loved Carla most never knew this comfort.

Weymouth wakes abruptly and lets the newspaper slide from his lap to the floor. "Bedtime for me," he announces. He drains the last of his drink and carries the glass to the kitchen. He reappears behind his wife's chair.

"I'll be up as soon as I finish this story," Carla says.

He puts his hands on the chair back, leans, rocks slightly over her.

"Really," she says. "You go ahead."

"Don't be long, babe."

She strokes one of his hands. "If I let his head touch the pillow, he's fast asleep," she says.

When Weymouth has gone up, we sit for several minutes without speaking. I sip from my drink; the house is silent.

"Should you keep him waiting?"

"It's all right." She puts the book aside. "Just the same, I'd better say good-night."

She throws off the quilt, comes over to my chair and leans to kiss me lightly on the forehead. "No more fairy tales," she says.

After she has gone to bed, I prop myself against the couch pillows and cover my legs with the lavender quilt Carla has nested in. My half-empty glass of bourbon sits on the window ledge behind the couch, its ice cubes melted so long ago that the outside of the glass is dry and I don't worry about leaving a ring on the dark wood.

When I get up the next morning, Weymouth has left for the city and Carla is out by the barn, graining the mare. I watch her from my bedroom window; from this distance, blue-jeaned and blue-shirted, she might be any ordinary country wife.

Downstairs, I pour a cup of the coffee left warming at the back of the stove, sit at the dining-room table to watch the dogs chasing something in the broad meadow on the other side of the garden, rummage through the kitchen desk to find paper to make some notes about my cellist. Chamber music is playing on the radio in the living room—*The Four Tempera- ments*, I think—and I realize I particularly notice the music because there has been none of it during my visit.

"Don't you play at all anymore?" I say after Carla has come inside and stands at the sink to wash.

She dries her hands and arms on the dish towel. "You're forgetting," she says. "I took the degree in literature."

"But all those years of piano?"

"What every well-bred lady does." She takes her wrist- watch from the counter beside the sink and fastens it on. "We'd better get moving, or you'll miss your flight."

In the car, after we have climbed the rain-carved road out of the hollow, Carla says, "Probably I use Clive as an excuse for quitting the music, when the real reason is my puny tal- ent. Anyway, I hardly touch the keyboard. I make Kate take lessons, of course. Or what's a mother for?"

"Poor Clive," I say.

"I was the one who found him, you know," Carla says.

"I thought it was his wife."

"No, lucky me. At about three in the morning. I'd been at a girlfriend's apartment, cramming for a biology exam—you remember that old-fashioned liberal arts program, where we all had to have a lab science even if we were terrible at it— and going back to campus, I went out of my way to walk past his house."

We are stopped for a moment at the traffic sign where the gravel road meets the blacktop. Off to the right, under strands of power lines, sits the trailer old Harley lives in. It has an added-on porch, and on the porch are a half-dozen black- and-white cats, all marked more or less alike, with black faces, black tails, black forelegs.

"I did that detour all the time," Carla says. "I don't know what I thought would happen. Perhaps that he'd see me and come outside and talk to me, invite me in. 'My wife's away; let's go to bed.' Something foolish like that. Or that I'd catch a glimpse of him through the parlor window, sitting at his piano, composing, dedicating the composition to me. I was terribly sentimental in my twenties, gushy and ripe for glamorous adventure."

"I don't remember you like that," I say. She is driving very fast on these roads that are like a snake's back.

"I changed," she says. "That morning changed me. A light was on in the kitchen, and another in the garage behind the house. I imagined Clive making coffee, starting the new day because his insomnia gave him no choice. I thought if I screwed up my courage and knocked at the back door he'd be pleased to see me, but I hadn't even gotten to the porch steps before I sensed something awful was happening. I could hear the car, I could see through the garage window that fog of automobile exhaust, I must have been screaming before I ever got to him."

She glances at me, as if I might say something, but she must know I'm beside her outside the garage, hearing the throb of the engine of Clive's white Opel, smelling the exhaust.

"It was bizarre," Carla says. "The first thing I saw, the very first, was that orange cat of his, curled up on the hood of the car, asleep. Only of course it was dead. And then I went into the garage and found Clive, lying on the floor in back of the car."

"I thought he was inside, in the driver's seat."

"No. He'd lain down as close as he could to the tailpipe; I suppose he wanted to drink from it. I got the doors open, dragged him outside—just took hold of his ankles and hauled him out to the lawn, but he was dead weight. It was like pulling I don't know what. Rolled-up carpet. Something. I knew he'd really done it, really killed himself."

She brings the car to a stop on the shoulder and rests her forehead against the top of the steering wheel. "You'd better drive," she says.

I wonder if she knows that Clive's will sent his body to a

research hospital in Boston, and that more than a year later his ashes came back to his widow. When I saw them, they were in a two-pound coffee can someone had painted flat black; you could just make out the brand name of the coffee through the paint. Marilyn scheduled a memorial service, gathered friends of Clive's from all over to mourn him a second time.

We met at a cemetery on the edge of town—it was June, deep green and shady and cool, with a breeze from the west that was barely strong enough to move smoke. A hole had been dug, a foot deep, perhaps ten inches square. The coffee can was passed around, each of us supposed to take a handful of ashes, to say something personal and appropriate and pour the ashes into the hole. It was dreadful. Clive's ashes were gritty and pale gray, with pebbles of black and white interspersed in the finer powder—I didn't know at the time how charcoal is added to the furnace to make the fire hotter—and when I put my hand into them I felt my stomach muscles clench for a terrible moment of revived grief.

By then, Carla was long gone, graduated and working in West Virginia; probably she had already met Weymouth.

"Please drive." She sits up. "I really can't see the damned road."

We wait in the airport coffee shop for my flight to be called. Carla's eyes are dry; she looks sheepish, as if it were not to be expected that a woman who works and digs potatoes and cares for horses should be guilty of tears.

"I wonder," she says, "when you look back on this visit, what will you most remember?"

"I'll certainly remember the girl on Quarrier."

For just a moment Carla looks disappointed; but then she says, "Of course, that's just your sort of thing—yours and Clive's and Wey's."

"You'd forgotten her?"

"Oh, no. I've thought more than once about that braid: the attention it must demand—so much work, and no reward except the admiration of strangers. And what a headache it must give her, all that burden."

"When you were at school," I say. "How long your hair was in those days."

"Those days," Carla says. She reaches across the table and takes my hands in hers—her pianist's hands, with the long competent fingers and the wide reach Clive raved about. "They're calling your flight."

"Yes."

She presses my hands and releases them. "You'll be in Boston before I get home."

"Even at Carla speed?"

She laughs. The laughter changes her face, makes her younger, reprises the student she was when I knew her in Vermont. As we walk to the gate she holds on to my arm and lets me feel her weight, catch the sweet, earthy smell of her clothes.

"Two things," she says. "Two things determine how long the hair can be: the strength of the roots and the strength of the person. My roots aren't very strong."

"But the other?"

"Ah, Walter," she says. We are at the gate; she puts two fingers to her mouth and conveys the kiss gracefully from her lips to mine. "In that, I hope I'm Rapunzel."

Sons

Whenever my Uncle Alton took me fishing he carried with him, in a polished black leather holster that rode just behind his left hip and against his skinny buttock, a large blued-steel army .45 pistol. I could hardly lift it. My uncle let me hold it once and encouraged me to aim it at some nearby target. To this day I remember the remarkable weight of it—the weapon trembling as I raised it in the direction of a birdhouse that dangled from the branches of the sugar maple in Aunt Dorothy's front yard, and, once I had gotten the birdhouse in my sights, my aim wavering and dipping and finally falling away as the pistol dropped to my side.

"The gun's too heavy," I said.

He took the pistol back from me, flicked the safety off and on again, and pushed it back into the holster. "It isn't a gun," he told me, his voice not entirely kind. "You never call it a gun. It's a weapon, or a piece, or a pistol. This particular weapon is also called a side arm."

"All right," I said.

"What is this?" He slapped at the holster. "What do we call it?"

"A side arm."

"That's the idea," he said. "Let's go catch some trout."

I was twelve then, spending the summer with Uncle Alton and Aunt Dorothy, and wherever Uncle Alton and I went, he carried the pistol with him. When we fished in the brook that cut across the meadow nearby, it was at his side. If we drove into Brunswick in his white Buick convertible, to buy a Sunday paper or a bottle of whiskey at the green front, the .45 lay wrapped in the leather of its holster and belt on the seat between us, and was locked into the glove compartment when we left the car. If we were only walking about the farm —which had been his father's, and seemed to have come down to him against his will, so that he despised it and had let the barns, the shed and the chicken coop weather and sag —he kept the pistol in hand, out of its black sheath. Sometimes he would stop, sight the weapon over the shirt sleeve of his left forearm, and fire off a single round in the direction of a crow on a ridgepole of the main barn or a rabbit bounding down a weedy garden furrow.

The very first time he fired the pistol when I was with him, I saw the brass shell case fly and catch the glint of sunlight, and I ran to pick it up.

"That's hot stuff," Uncle Alton said, just as I touched my fingers to it and discovered that it was.

He knelt beside me and let me hold a loaded cartridge on my flattened palm, showing me the brass case with the silver-colored circle in its base where the firing pin struck, and the copper slug that flew to the target. He explained to me about the black-powder explosion that sent the slug on its way.

"And then you feel the kick," he said. "When the bullet goes forward, there's an equal force that shoves backward, against your arm and shoulder. That's why you squeeze a trigger—you never pull it—so you don't add any more uncertainty to your aim, and that's why with a weapon this powerful you start your aim a little above the target and bring it slowly down. That way, you're already compensating for the recoil, the kick."

I nodded, believing I understood exactly what he was saying.

I once watched Uncle Alton shoot at a fish. It was a later summer, far too sultry for Maine—an August afternoon, dog days, the sound of locusts a whine like an electric saw. We were crossing the meadow behind the farm, on our way to the Cumberland County Power & Light Company dam, whose reservoir was stocked with speckled trout. My uncle strode ahead, with his fly-casting rod in his right hand. His wicker creel lay against his right hip, the holster of the pistol against his left. In the crook of my left arm was a coffee can, its bottom seething with worms I had dug out of my aunt's garden in the cool of early morning.

I trailed behind. I had a telescoping metal rod, brand-new, with red-jeweled eyelets the line fed through, and a fancy new reel I never did learn the knack of. I'm not much of a fisherman now, but I was worse then, and on that day I was miserable—sullen because my new fishing gear wasn't fly tackle, like Uncle Alton's, and dreading the prospect of sitting on the edge of the pond to thread a barbed hook through another innocent worm.

We were walking alongside Stimpson's Brook, a spring-fed stream whose current was slow and whose color was the yellow-green of the sun playing through tall grasses along its banks. A mile or so from the dam, Uncle Alton stopped and put back a hand to warn me into silence.

"Look there," he whispered.

I crept up beside him and looked. The water here was eight

or nine feet across—a kind of resting-place for the stream, a
deep pool landscaped with rocks of various sizes, where the
current paused and eddied before resuming its purpose toward
the dam. Where my uncle pointed was a flat rock jutting into
the center of this pool, and there in the shadow of the rock
was a fish.

"Pickerel," Uncle Alton said. "Four pounds if he's an
ounce."

The pickerel seemed to me enormous—slender and sub-
marine-shaped, with a head tapering into jaws that seemed
too small for its size. It idled under the edge of the outcrop-
ping, its tail moving ever so slightly—just enough, I supposed, to keep it in place in the shade.

"Are we going to catch him?" I whispered.

"Let me have that coffee can," my uncle said. He laid his
fly rod in the grass and took the worm can from me. He
changed leaders on his line and skewered one of my worms
onto a bare hook, then stood up slowly—the sun was on the
other side of the brook, so no shadow fell across the lazy
pickerel—and lowered the line into the water.

The fish seemed oblivious. Uncle Alton held the line at
arm's length and steered it in front of the pickerel. Nothing.
He moved the line—the poor worm still writhing on its steel
point of agony—around the motionless fish, then upward, so
that the worm actually brushed the mottled skin of the pickerel's near side. The pickerel let its tail weave a slow figure-8
for stability, but seemed otherwise unperturbed.

Not so my uncle. "The devil," he said very softly.

"I guess he's not hungry," I remember saying.

"I guess not," Uncle Alton agreed. He drew out the line
and got the worm off the hook. "You can put this back in the
can."

I backed off. "It's all bloody," I said.

He gave me a puzzled look, then tossed the worm into the
pool. I watched it sink, coiling and uncoiling in the sunlit
water, falling to the sandy bottom squarely across the pickerel's field of vision. Perhaps the fish was blind, I thought.

When I took my attention away from the stream, Uncle Alton had unsnapped his holster and was aiming the .45 into the brook. He clicked off the safety and squeezed the trigger.

Two echoes followed: the one the explosion, like thunder, of the firing pin meeting the cartridge; the other the singing of the bullet, whose trajectory took too shallow an angle and whose ricochet away from the disturbed surface of the water was a sound I had heard only in Saturday-afternoon cowboy films. I was stunned by what my uncle had done.

"The devil," he said again, this time at normal volume, for both of us could see that the noise of the shot had not budged the pickerel. Uncle Alton stepped to the edge of the brook and fired a second time. This time the bullet entered the pool with a great burbling sound and spent itself—we could see its downward bending—long before it reached the pickerel.

We stood in silence, staring into the green shade that bathed the motionless fish.

"We better get a move on," my uncle said, and holstered the pistol.

For most of his active life, Uncle Alton was Scoggin's water commissioner, a job that absorbed him entirely when he was not in the field with tackle or weapon. He was what used to be known as "a man's man," and he had no patience with anyone on a job who fell short of what he expected. Even during the long summer days when I was on hand to observe him, my uncle left for work at dawn and was hardly ever home before dark. He smelled of earth—the same earth that caught under his nails and prompted Aunt Dorothy to send him, night after night, back to the sink to wash as an example to me and to the other children.

He had four daughters, and though they doted on him—and clearly, he loved them as much as any father can love his children—there was in his manner with them a deliberate reserve. It was as if he were afraid of breaking something fragile, and so when they hugged him, or flew into his lap while he sat pondering the town's flawed drainage systems, or begged him to let them go to dances and parties arranged by their school friends, he would be wary of touching them. He listened to them as one listens to foreigners, careful not to embarrass them by failing to recognize a word they have mispronounced. He answered them solemnly, like a judge handing down a verdict.

To my knowledge, he never took any of his daughters fishing or hunting. Yet he hated to be alone in the outdoors, and so every summer I became Uncle Alton's son, supposedly to be taught those manly arts. I imagine I was a constant disappointment to him—no more apt than a girl might have been with pistols and rifles, with wicked hunting knives, with fishing rods whose slender lines snarled in reels my thumb was too slow to manipulate properly—though usually he was patient with me. If I angered him, he was more likely than not to curse my mother or my schoolteacher father for their failure to encourage my interest in the active life.

My mother was his sister; from my eleventh birthday onward, they argued about me when we all gathered at the Scoggin farm for Thanksgiving dinner.

"Why do you sissify the boy?" Uncle Alton would say. Almost any gesture of my mother's might provoke him: her habit of reaching over to brush the hair back from my forehead, or bending to kiss me lightly on the cheek when I was near her, or sitting me beside her on the piano bench while she played and sang Ethelbert Nevin's "Mighty Lak a Rose." "What are you trying to make him into?"

Then would begin the debate over whether or not I should be allowed to go deer hunting at Jackman with Uncle Alton and his closest friends—"your cronies" my mother called them. The older I got, the worse the argument. When I was in my early teens, Mother was adamant: certainly I could not go; it was out of the question. I was given to understand that the atmosphere of the hunting camp, its rowdiness and profanity, its coarse jokes and the presence of whiskey and gin, justified her objection.

"It's no place for a nice boy," she told me.

My father was silent; he was a great reader of newspapers and of *Life* magazine, and every Thanksgiving he settled himself behind whichever was handier. The possibility of my killing a wild animal, of proving my manhood in such a way as to satisfy Uncle Alton, seemed of no moment to my natural father.

When I turned fifteen, the tone of my mother's misgivings changed. "Ask your father" was all she would say. But when I went to him, he studied me over his lowered *Boston Post* as if I were a stranger and a perplexity.

"It's up to your mother," he said, and disappeared behind the newspaper.

In fact, I never hunted. It was just as well, for though I was entranced by my uncle's collection of weapons—besides the .45, he owned a .357 Magnum, .30-30 and .30-06 rifles for deer hunting, a .22-caliber target pistol, two or three .22 rifles, and a brace of shotguns for ducks and skeet shooting— I was never very good with any of them, and not drawn to the responsibility of pointing them at a living creature. But the idea of the weapons attracted me, and the saying of their names: "thirty aught-six" and "three fifty-seven Magnum" and "twelve-gauge over-and-under." I was a poor marksman, the bane of Uncle Alton's life as a surrogate father, but I became adept at the vocabulary of shooting.

Only once, just before my sixteenth birthday, did I try to buy a weapon—a side arm—of my own. It was an exquisite, delicate-looking Beretta pistol, .25-caliber, its handle inlaid with mother-of-pearl, and I had seen it in a glass case at the front of Shaw's Hardware alongside several other handguns of lesser beauty. I cannot say why I so wanted the Beretta, except that when I held it in my hand I felt all at once adult, and when I put down my fifteen-dollar deposit, a strength that was genuinely physical surged through my adolescent muscles.

My new sense of maturity and power was short-lived. Willard Shaw telephoned to ask if my father approved of the

purchase, and of course my father, ignorant of everything, did
not. I came into the house just as the conversation ended.

"Thanks for calling, Bill," my father was saying. "You can
be darned sure I'll put the kibosh on that."

I expect Uncle Alton might have forgiven my incompetence
if years later I had somehow made a man—hunter, camper,
woodsman—of my own son. But though Jonathan grew to be
taller and stronger than I had ever been, he failed to win over
my uncle. Once, after his retirement, Uncle Alton came to
visit us in Syracuse. It was several years since he had seen
Jonathan—who was now fourteen and lanky and wore his
blond hair to his shoulders in the style of the day—and I
thought for a moment or two he was on the verge of apoplexy.

"What the devil are you?" he said to poor Jonathan. "Are
you a boy or a goddamned girl?"

Less than a week earlier, the McDonald's where Jonathan
worked—his first job—had been robbed by two armed men.
Just at closing, one of the men had surprised Jonathan in the
parking lot, jammed a sawed-off shotgun into his ribs, and
forced him back inside the restaurant. A second man sat the
employees on the floor behind the counter and held a hand-
gun on them, while the first collected the day's receipts. Jonathan was interviewed on the next evening's television news.
He was soft-spoken, articulate, somewhat ironic about the
whole business. I don't know why I didn't tell all this to my
uncle, or show him the ugly bruise the shotgun made when it
was poked into Jonathan's ribs; perhaps I didn't want to hum-
ble him.

Later in the week Alton asked to be taken golfing. I walked
the course with him, caddying, and listened to what he had
to say about the flaws in his world. He was retired as Scoggin's
water commissioner, and still bitter about the way "a green
college boy" had been hired, fresh out of M.I.T., to replace
him.

"They call me up, you know," Alton said. "He gets into holes he can't dig himself out of, and his books don't tell him squat, and sure as goddamned hell one of the selectmen rings my phone at five in the morning to bail the town out."

"But that should flatter you," I said.

He measured a twelve-footer, then watched it rim the cup. He stood for a moment, studying the line of the putt as if he could draw the ball back for a second try. Then he said, "Don't be flattered when a fellow tells you you're the best man for the job. You never know how rotten the competition was."

Afterward, in the clubhouse, where he nursed a bottle of Narragansett and we watched through the picture window as a foursome of women teed off at number one, Uncle Alton apologized to me.

"I shouldn't have picked on your boy," he said. "I don't know what gets into me. Your Aunt Dottie—she tries to muzzle me, God knows. Tells me I'm too quick on the trigger."

"You don't like men to be soft," I said.

He shook his head. "I never got a son," he said. "I never knew what the knack of it was." He refilled his glass from the bottle and let the head foam up and over the rim; then he lifted the glass and swept the puddle of spilled beer off the table with the side of his hand. "That father of yours," Alton said. "He did it. You did it. What's the trick?"

"It's just luck," I said.

Alton sipped his beer. "I could have made something of you," he said. And then he grinned—a broad grin, probably full of whatever he remembered of the times I had spent with him. "God knows what," he said.

There was a killing in Portland. I never knew the details, except that the weather was unusually warm—the kind of day it had been when I watched Uncle Alton shoot at the pickerel in Stimpson's Brook—and the incident had grown out of a trivial argument over a loud stereo. Two policemen intervened in the quarrel, called by neighbors, and one of them was shot dead. The murderer was a shipyard worker from New Hampshire, who fled in his car, driving north on I-95, crashing through a roadblock, then leaving the interstate at Freeport to follow narrow roads inland until he ran out of gas. A state trooper found the car abandoned near Scoggin.

While he was still water commissioner Uncle Alton had been made an honorary sheriff's deputy, and he had never given up the honor. His new Buick carried a sheriff's-department decal on its rear bumper, and I knew from my rare visits to the Scoggin farm that he kept a red roof lamp between the front seats—"They call it a gum ball," he told me when he showed it to me—and that the .45 was still in the glove compartment, snug in its black leather holster. Of course he joined the manhunt—it was in his back yard, wasn't it? he told Aunt Dorothy—and he drove to the place where the car had been discovered.

Within a couple of hours, he was far away from the main area of the search—far from the troopers and sheriff's people tramping warily through tall grasses, far from the helicopters circling overhead—and he stopped to rest and get his bearings. He was tired—he was in his seventies, remember—and he was hot and thirsty and had begun to realize that, deputy or no deputy, he wasn't being much help to the manhunt. He decided to walk back to his car and go home.

He had not gone far when he heard a noise, "like a twig snapping under a boot." He crouched, drew his pistol, and moved toward the sound. At some point, he released the safety catch. Telling Aunt Dorothy about it later, he couldn't recall exactly when he had done that, but the catch was off when he came to a stone wall laid at the edge of a woodlot. As he was climbing over the wall, a stone gave way under him and he fell; the pistol flew out of his hand and struck the ground. When it discharged, the bullet caught Uncle Alton in the left leg, just above the knee.

"I don't know how he made it home," Aunt Dorothy said over the phone a few days afterward. "The bone is splintered and he lost an awful lot of blood, and the front seat and the carpeting of that poor Buick is just a mess, but here he came up the driveway, like a soldier boy home from the wars. Dr. Ross says he's not sure he can save the leg."

"Can I talk to him?"

"I think you'd better not," Aunt Dorothy said. "He hasn't uttered a civil word since the accident."

The leg couldn't be saved; and several months later I saw Uncle Alton for the last time. I was appalled by how much he had changed, how shrunken he seemed. Neither of us mentioned his accident. But it was not as if the manhunt had never happened; I think he was obsessed by it, and he would fall into long silences that changed his face and made his eyes enormously sad. He no longer drank—not even light beer or ale—but he was allowed two cups of coffee a day, and the two of us sat in the kitchen of the farmhouse while Aunt Dorothy fussed over us, bringing not only coffee but fresh cream and blueberry muffins hot from the oven.

"How long since you've been down East?" Alton asked me. "Three, four years?"

"Closer to five," I said.

"I thought so," he said.

"I see you tore down that old barn."

"The wind took it down," Alton said. "It's nothing I did."

Aunt Dorothy caught my eye and shook her head. Don't remind him how helpless he feels, her look said.

"Well, it's a big improvement," I said.

"What do you remember best about this place?" he said. "Be honest, now."

I thought. "I suppose learning to shoot," I said. "And the day you let me handle that forty-five of yours that I could barely lift."

"Oh, yes," he said.

"I remember I called it a 'gun,' " I said.

"Oh, yes." He turned to speak over his shoulder to Aunt Dorothy. "Get that for me, will you, Dot? You know where it is."

She left the two of us in the kitchen. I took a sip of coffee; Uncle Alton sat silently, his fingers drumming on what remained of his left leg.

"Jonathan's just finished his master's degree," I said.

Alton nodded and smiled. "That long hair of his," he said. "I could never figure how they'd let him work around food with that hair as long as a girl's."

"That was years ago," I said. "He wore a hair-net."

Uncle Alton's face registered first surprise, then amusement. "The devil," he said.

When Aunt Dorothy came back and handed him the familiar .45 in its black holster, he passed it across the table to me and labored up from the chair onto his crutches. "Let's take a little stroll," he said. "You won't have any trouble keeping up."

"Oh, Al," Aunt Dorothy said.

"It's all right, Dottie. Don't nag at me."

I followed him out to the hall and walked down the back steps beside him.

"She hates what she calls my gloom-and-doom," Alton said. "She seems to think I should be happy to have one leg."

"It's better than none, isn't it?"

He gave me a deprecating glance. "You're your father's son," he said.

We crossed the back lot, past what was left of the barn—I could see that some of the old boards were cradled like a fallen ruin inside the granite walls—and we seemed to be headed toward the chicken coop. There hadn't been chickens in a long time, I knew. Aunt Dorothy had tried to raise them for profit after Alton left the water commissioner's job, but he'd complained so much about the noise and stench that she had to give it up—"for the sake of my sanity," she told me. But the smell was still there, and the air around the coop sang with the buzz of flies whose green bodies glistened in the sunlight.

We stopped beside the coop. Alton set the crutches against the wall of it and put his left hand on its roof. "Boost me up," he said.

It was a low roof, not more than five feet off the ground, but it was no easy matter to help a one-legged, seventy-five-year-old man climb onto it. I put the .45 on the ground behind me and struggled with my uncle, finally managing to get him up there. He dragged himself into a sitting position, overlooking the chicken-wire enclosure of the hen yard, and settled himself.

"Now the pistol," he said.

I picked it up from the ground and passed it to him. He unsnapped the holster and slid out the .45, then he released the clip and checked to see that it was full. It was, and he reloaded the pistol.

"You could do me a favor," he said. "You could go back to the house and get that box of cartridges in the kitchen drawer just to the left of the refrigerator."

"What are you going to do?" I said.

He clicked off the safety and pointed the .45 down into the hen yard where scores of fat flies moved on the hard ground. "Big game," he said. "You see the one in the corner? Right beside that straight twig?"

He fired. The fly was gone in a puff of dust; there was a wide hole in the earth where it had been.

"Go get those cartridges," Alton said. "I'll be fine."

I trudged back to the house. Behind me, the noise of the .45 exploded into the summer silence again and again. All the time I was out of his sight, I was afraid of the worst; I expected the worst; but when I got back to the chicken coop with the cartridge box heavy in my hand, Uncle Alton was still alive, drawing a bead on another fat fly with a weapon that needed reloading.

In fact, Uncle Alton died in his sleep a few months later. At
the funeral, Aunt Dorothy told me that for years she and the
girls had worried about how he would die, and that the peace-
fulness of his actual death was all she could have wished for.
How was my son, Jonathan? she wondered. What was he
doing since college? Did I think he was happy with life on his
own?

Favorites

On a Saturday afternoon in September his wife was killed in a car accident. As the state police explained it to him, she had finished her grocery shopping and was pulling out onto the highway in front of the shopping center when a young man in a pickup truck slammed into her car. The impact was just behind the driver's door; she died instantly, never knew what hit her—things people say in such circumstances, things the police told him. The young man wasn't hurt; he was drunk and stoned, and charges against him were pending. Very sorry. The car was written off as a total loss.

For a time he felt terribly guilty. Once the shock had passed and he had accepted everyone's sympathy, once he had phoned her parents and made the funeral arrangements, once he found himself alone for the first time with a tumbler of bourbon in his hand, he believed he had killed her by wishing her dead. He remembered all the times when she had been late coming home, especially in bad weather, and he had imagined the worst. He remembered being absorbed in spite of himself by television movies in which husbands plotted with mistresses to murder wives. He remembered how some-times, even at fifty years old, he would see a young woman whose mouth or eyes or competent hands exerted upon him an attraction that was nearly unbearable, and he would think: If I had no wife.

In all such reveries he played the action out. How would he be told of her death? How would he respond? What would he say, do, feel? It was like rehearsing for a scene at the community playhouse. Except that at the fall of the curtain he caught himself up, and said to himself: What the hell is the matter with you? And he said to God, fervently: Dear God, I don't want her to die; don't pay any attention to my thoughts.

It was true that he didn't want her to die—so true that when it actually happened it was as if he had never walked through a rehearsal, had a bloody daydream, or fantasied an-other woman. He broke down completely. Later he was able to talk only in stammers. Later still he had to be instructed what calls to make, and as he made them he kept giving way to tears. Finally—when the funeral was over and his wife's casket was covered with dirt and the friends and relatives were dispersed—he saw that it was self-indulgent to take the blame for her death, and he admitted to himself that he was not guilty after all.

The day after the funeral service he decided to reorder his life in such a way as to account for his solitary condition. He began in the kitchen. First he went through the cupboards: he threw out all the diet foods—the peaches, the candies, the sugar substitutes; he threw out the tins of connoisseur coffees whose flavors he had never liked; he threw out his wife's coffee mug, realizing how sentimental a gesture it prob-ably was, and while he was at it he got rid of the cracked

Pyrex measuring cup whose red graduation marks had long ago begun to wear off. When he went through the kitchen drawers, he pulled out all the tools and utensils whose use he had never understood, the dish towels made of a fabric that always seemed to smear the glasses without drying them, the clumsy pot holders woven by nieces and cousins and the daughters of friends, the fancy chromed corkscrew that continually defeated him. He cleared every surface: counter, sideboard, the table in the breakfast nook, the top of the refrigerator, the window seat where the cat liked to sleep— potted plants, mostly, he disposed of. Everything went into the trash cans in the garage, and the trash cans went out to the curb.

He cleaned out the refrigerator last. Ice cream, cocktail snacks, potato chips, more fancy coffees—all of these items in opened bags and cartons, nibbled at, half-gone— he cleared out of the freezer compartment. Below, he disposed of vegetables already going to rot, beef liver he knew he would not cook in time, jars of dressings, and plastic containers whose contents he could not identify. Pitchers of orange juice and iced tea . . . My God, he kept thinking, I have an entire house to go through. Cheese slices he did not like, salami he would not eat—he stripped the shelves bare.

At the very bottom of the refrigerator was a covered metal cake pan. He slid it out, popped up the lid, and saw what it contained. Much later—perhaps for the rest of his life—he would recall the extraordinary effect of this last discovery. It changed the light in the kitchen, it altered his balance so profoundly that he could not stand without the support of the kitchen counter, and it sharpened the edges of every object in view. Whatever seeds of guilt, of remorse, of lonely terror he had lately felt, they flowered over again as he remembered the last words his wife ever said to him:

"I made your favorite dessert."

For the next couple of weeks he was "looked after" by friends. They called him when he got home from work and invited him to the movies. They took him to dinner—sometimes to a better restaurant with cloth napkins; sometimes, for a lark, to a McDonald's or a Burger King. Once a close chum of his wife's coaxed him to have lunch at a new Chinese restaurant, where the food was only so-so, but the waiters were extravagantly attentive. He could see what was coming, where his friends were leading him. One day he would find himself sitting across from an attractive widow or divorcée—a well-kept woman perhaps three or four years younger than his wife. One night he would be out on a blind date. The prospect of falling into the hands of matchmakers did not appeal to him, but these were friends: he went along. If they forced matters too far, he would have to protest gently.

He decided to eat the dessert his wife had left him. Once he came to terms with the realization that her last words were so trivial—it seemed to him a farewell that mocked the importance of their marriage and love—he saw no sense either to putting the dessert down the garbage-disposal or to pretending it was a symbol of the irony of existence. It was what it was: a rich, delicious afterpiece. A benign bad habit. Sweet vice.

The dessert was a concoction of vanilla pudding and whipped cream, laid down in alternating layers between a bottom crust of pastry and a topping of chocolate frosting. It truly was his favorite; it was like éclairs and cream puffs and French pastry horns all in one. Sweet and rich though it was, it was deceptively light. Sometimes he indulged in a second helping, yet the dessert never made him feel logy, nor did it provoke the conscience of the middle-aged man who knows he is getting doughy around the waist. Even when he avoided seconds, he tried to draw out the eating of the dessert. He invariably saved it for the end of the evening. He savored it by letting each forkful melt in his mouth, swallowing not the food, but the elixir distilled from it. He thought this dessert had taught him something of Plato.

His wife, pleading calories, never touched it. It amused him that she seemed so much to enjoy making the confection for him, and at the same time was adamant about its danger to herself. It was very like a paradox. He used to tease her: Why won't you taste it? Is it poisoned? Are you trying to get rid of me? Sometimes she had played the part with him: Yes, oh God, I confess; you've found me out. And he said: I've given some to the cat. If this cat keels over, it's the gas chamber for you, Lucrezia.

All of that seemed horrible now. I'd rather have a fat wife than no wife, he told himself as he cut the first piece of her last dessert. And then, seeing what a mess he was making with the knife at the corner of the pan, he remembered the joke he had made up for her, years ago.

Q. Why is this dessert like a car on a cold day?

A. Because it's hard to start.

He considered the plate in his hand—it held a shapeless disorder of dark chocolate and pale vanilla—and felt his grief all over again.

At the beginning he was prodigal with the dessert. When he arrived home from the movie or the dinner with friends, he cut himself a man-sized serving and carried the plate into the living room to watch the television news or Johnny Carson. The sweetness of the dessert made his wife's presence vivid to him; as he indulged his appetite, his memory indulged the past. More than once he realized that he had been watching five minutes of weather, yet had no inkling of the forecast. Lying in the dark in his empty bed he could not recall the important news stories, though he had listened to all of them. He was scarcely aware of the guests on the Carson show, unless one of them was an actress who reminded him—by her face, her carriage, some small gesture or inflection—of his wife, and then it was never the guest's words that he heard, but his wife's, discussing the dessert.

"I've got a new treat for you. I cut the recipe out of a magazine."

That first time, he had gone to the kitchen to see. He watched her spoon out each filling, one layer at a time, and spread it with a rubber spatula. He imagined the strata building under her hand; his mouth watered. "Geologist of sugar" he once called his wife.

After the first week the dessert was more than half gone, and he wondered if he shouldn't try to make it last. One day he had eaten two helpings—it was a Saturday and he felt a craving for it in the afternoon while he was watching baseball. Certainly he could be somewhat less lavish. The next time he cut a modest helping. He used the tine of his fork to outline future pieces, making the rectangles smaller. He imagined he heard his wife saying: "Why aren't you eating that fancy dessert? If it's in the refrigerator too long it starts to weep."

He ate as slowly as he could, thinking about that curious meaning of the word "weep."

One night only a single piece of his wife's dessert remained. He cut it in half. The following night he cut the half in half. Then he must have realized what he was doing, for on the third night he ate all that was left of the dessert—luscious, irreplaceable treat—and set the empty pan to soak in the kitchen sink.

Terrible Kisses

December. On the twenty-fourth, Harris Calder will celebrate his fortieth birthday, and Maureen, his lover, wants to do something memorable to mark the day. What her gift will be, Harris cannot imagine, and though Maureen moves through the days leading up to the birthday with a secret smile playing at the corners of her mouth, she gives him no clues.

They work in the same downtown bank, Consolidated Federal Trust, Harris as a loan officer and Maureen as a clerk in the safety deposit section, and they can just glimpse each other across the bank's broad main lobby—if Harris leans to the left to get a clear view past the frame of his cubicle, and if Maureen raises herself up a few inches to see over the sign on the counter that reads BOXHOLDERS STOP HERE.

Their colleagues are charmed by them, considering Harris and Maureen a perfect couple. In fact, the two have lived together for nearly a year, commencing the week after Harris's divorce. First he moved into Maureen's apartment, and then, because the apartment was too small, they talked to Ferdie Allerton in the mortgage section. Ferdie knew about a pending foreclosure—a nice little Cape Cod in the suburbs—and as soon as the paperwork was taken care of, the lovers moved in with two cats, a modest amount of Danish furniture, and a small German car. Such happy circumstances; they are the envy of all.

The birthday arrives. CFT closes its doors at noon for the holidays; Harris and Maureen meet in the cloakroom, where he helps her into her fake-fur jacket.

"Is it animal, vegetable, or mineral?" Harris asks, but Maureen keeps silent and puts out her lower lip in a mock pout. It is as if she knows that his ignorance makes her gift, whatever it is, more precious.

On the bus that takes them home, Harris studies Maureen's young profile—the small, perfect nose, the ripe lower lip, the jaw that is strong but not too strong—trying to read her. Walking from the bus stop to the house, he holds her gloved left hand and hums Christmas carols, watching his breath cloud the crisp air with music. On the front step he unlocks the door and ushers Maureen into the hallway. She turns to him then, hugs him and kisses him on the mouth.

"My birthday man," she says.

He shivers. "I love your kisses," he tells her.

"I know." She repeats the kiss. Then she hangs her jacket in the hall closet and starts toward the kitchen. "Why don't you take a nice hot shower," she says, "and then I'll make us a drink?"

When he finishes his shower, Maureen is seated at the dressing table, wearing the white chenille robe she has owned since her college days. Her bare legs suggest she is wearing only the robe, and Harris feels an echo of the shiver her kisses provoked in the downstairs hall.

"How about that drink?" he says.

"In a minute."

Harris sees that she is leaning into the dressing-table mirror, putting on lipstick. He sits on the bed and towels his damp hair distractedly.

"I thought you didn't use makeup," he says.

"Not usually. A little mascara, so my eyes don't look so piggy-tiny." She blots her mouth with a pale-blue tissue and studies the imprint she has made.

"So why the lipstick?"

She shakes her head. "It's part of your surprise," she says. "But I don't know which shade to use."

"Let me help," Harris says. He prides himself on his judgment in aesthetic matters. "How many choices?"

"Just two." She holds up the lipsticks—gold-colored tubes with extended narrow tongues of pale red.

"They look the same."

"No," Maureen says. "Come over here."

He stands before her. She pushes his bathrobe aside and plants a firm kiss over his left nipple. "This one is called Bon-Bonfire," she says. She scrubs at her lips with a tissue, then watches her reflection apply color from the other tube. She presses a second kiss above his right nipple. "And this one is Coral Blaze."

He holds the lapels of the robe apart and studies the impressions of her kisses, which look like small, symmetrical wounds on his chest. No, they are more like vivid parachutes his nipples are riding down into the curly forest of his hair. Or do they seem to be curious watermarks on the parchment of his damp skin?

"They look the same," he says.

Maureen sighs. "No," she says. She touches the imprint on the left side. "This is more pink. The other is a sort of pale magenta."

"I think I prefer the magenta," Harris says.

"Good," Maureen says. "So do I." She freshens the gloss already on her lips. "Now you have to take off your bathrobe and lie down for me."

* * *

She begins at the soles of his feet, kissing the left, then the right, pausing to put on new lipstick, kissing left and right, pausing again, until Harris sees—propped on his elbows to watch—that she intends to cover him with kisses. The prints of her lips blanket his feet and ankles like a pattern as pronounced as argyle, and the pattern moves slowly up his legs —to his knees, his thighs, his groin. He thinks she will stop there, having made her affection for him visible, and that now the two of them will make love—that this is the birthday gift, symbolic and real at the same time, she has been planning all along.

"You really know how to drive a man crazy," he says.

She is kneeling beside him, refreshing the lipstick, and she smiles at his words. "It takes a lot of time," she says. "I have to reapply the color every couple of kisses, or else they won't be bright enough."

"They certainly are bright," Harris concedes. Looking down the length of his body, he feels like a freak in a sideshow, the multiplied images of Maureen's mouth opening all over his legs like tattoo-parlor roses. "Now let me put my arms around you," he says, reaching.

"Not yet," she says.

Instead, he is obliged to turn onto his stomach, and now she prints her kisses up the backs of his legs—left, right, pause, left, right—over his buttocks, along his spine, across his shoulder blades. It is like no birthday gift he could have imagined. Alicia, his ex-wife, would never have thought it up; no other woman in his life could have invented it, devised it, carried it out. His skin burns with the touch of Maureen's tender mouth. He thinks he can discriminate each individual kiss, each tiny nerve end the warmth of the lipstick balances on. He has never been so sensitized, and no lover has ever been so attentive to him.

"Now on your back," she says.

And he rolls over without question or hesitation, to let

Maureen finish what she has begun. He closes his eyes. Over his stomach and chest and throat and face her kisses pour like gouts of cinnamoned honey, like overripe strawberries leaving their sticky mark wherever they touch. His very eyelids are heavy with her imprint. His shoulders, his arms and wrists, the palms of his hands—Maureen leaves her pouting mouth on his every surface, in his every fold and corner. It is a process that seems to be taking hours, but when it is done it seems to have taken no time at all.

"I had to use some of the other color," Maureen says at last. "I ran out of the Coral Blaze." And finally she lies down beside him.

By the time they finish lovemaking, the bed linens are a pattern of pale kisses, as is Maureen's white robe—and Maureen herself is mostly decorated with the faint lip-shapes her lover's weight has pressed against her skin. As for Harris, the cloak of Maureen's myriad kisses glows as brightly as at first; he is from head to toe a perfect lithograph of passion.

"I hope you never forget this birthday," Maureen says. She lies beside him, leaning on one elbow, touching one or another of her imprinted kisses randomly and lightly with her free hand.

"I'll never," Harris says. "Never in a hundred years."

The kisses do not wash off. In the morning, while Maureen sleeps and the cats eat tuna and milk, Harris stands in the shower, soaps and soaps again. Though the kisses seem at first to fade in the general glow of the hot shower, he realizes when he has toweled dry and leaned into the mirror to shave that his skin still carries the marks of Maureen's patient gift. The kisses are like a pale flush on his cheeks and throat; his brow looks feverish. The backs of his hands as he raises them to his face bear the faint rosettes of Maureen's half-parted lips.

This is a strange persistence, Harris thinks. He puts his

hands under the cold-water tap and scrubs them with the
harsh soap he keeps to remove grease when he has worked on
the car. The coarse lather leaves his hands ruddy, but the
pattern of kisses remains. On Maureen's side of the medicine
chest he finds a jar of cold cream and rubs some of the goop
into his hands and forearms, then he wipes it off with facial
tissues. The tissues take on a greasy pink tinge, but his skin
does not come clear.

"Maureen," he whispers to the mirror. "Maureen," he says
out loud, and goes to the bedroom.

She rolls over to face him.

"Look," he says. He holds out his arms to her, his bathrobe
open to show the rust-colored design on his body.

"I know," she says. "You're lovely."

"No," he says. "Look at me."

"I see you. You're still wearing the red birthday suit I gave
you."

"It isn't funny," he says. "The kisses won't go away." His
voice breaks like a teen-aged boy's.

Maureen sits up in the bed. "Come here," she says. She
takes his left hand in hers and draws it into focus. She puts
her fingers to her mouth and rubs saliva on the back of the
hand. She purses her lips and frowns.

"You see?" Harris says plaintively.

"Look in the drawer to the right of the bathroom sink and
bring me that little pumice stone. And a wet washcloth."

"This is so weird," Harris says. He brings the pumice. "This
is crazy."

Maureen scours his arm with the rough stone. "Nothing's
happening," she says.

"I tingle," Harris says.

"Where I rubbed with the pumice?"

"All over," he says. "I tingle all over."

And it's true. It is as if his skin is dancing under the weight
of the kisses, as if the kisses are alive and sing through his
pores to his listening blood. It seems his whole body has

become the instrument of Maureen's impetuous and beautiful kisses.

"Dear heaven," Harris groans, "what am I going to do?" and he falls helplessly onto the bed beside Maureen.

No matter what he does, no matter what Maureen suggests, the kisses remain. Between Christmas and New Year's, while Maureen works at CFT, Harris uses vacation time to stay at home with the cats and grapple with his problem. He tries everything. He drinks liquids and buries himself under layers of blankets, hoping to sweat away the kisses as he might break a fever. He burns himself with caustics—bleaches and paint removers and drain cleaners—but gets nothing for his trouble except pain and blisters. He lies under sunlamps; his skin turns Florida-gold, and the kisses darken to bronze. He uses emery and sandpaper, he rubs his face with fish oil and gets the cats to lick him with their rough tongues, he applies lotions and dyes and stains. He scrapes at his flesh with such force that he draws blood—but when new skin appears, it bears freshened kisses to mock his labors. The tingling grows worse, deeper and hotter, until by the end of the year he cannot sit or lie or be quiet anywhere. He paces endlessly, as if he might somehow walk away from the agony of the kisses, but he wears that agony like perverse clothing. He feels like a man living in a tragedy excessively Greek. He wonders how it will all end. He wonders if he will have to kill himself in order to be free.

On the day after New Year's he goes back to the bank. Maureen spends an hour preparing him, covering the kisses on his face and neck and hands with makeup base so no one will know what has happened to him. The face he sees in the mirror is like a clever mask; the image is not Harris Calder, though it resembles him.

"They'll know," he says to Maureen. He holds out his hands as if they do not belong to him. "They'll see."

"I told them you've been ill," she says. "A rash. An allergic reaction."

To love, Harris thinks. I'm a man allergic to love.

At CFT, his colleagues seem pleased at his return, ask him how he feels, say they hope his rash is better. "All that rich Christmas food," Ferdie Allerton tells him. "Plum pudding; Tom and Jerry."

"No doubt," Harris says. All day he processes bill-payer loans while Maureen's fierce kisses burn under his clothes, under the tight mask of makeup, like a persistent guilty secret. He feels like a man on fire. It is all he can do to wait for the end of the banking day.

That night, he tells Maureen he is quitting CFT.

"I have to go away," he says. "I have to hide out until whatever is happening to me stops happening."

"Where will you go?"

"I'll find work where nobody knows me," Harris says. "I'll be an auto mechanic or a carpenter. I'll get a job in a booth on the tollway."

"What about me?" She puts her arms around Harris and holds him. The kisses on his body are like a thousand mouths that open to breathe in her embrace. "What will I do by myself?"

"I'll leave tomorrow, while you're at the bank," Harris says. Gently, he disengages himself from her arms. "When you come home, I'll be gone. After a while, you won't even miss me."

"Please stay," she whispers.

"I can't."

All night he lies on his back, staring up into the black sky of the bedroom. Maureen is beside him; sometimes she sleeps, sometimes she wakes to plead with him. Her tears on his face feel cold beside the fever of her kisses. He wishes his skin were a thin shirt he could take off and fold and put away in the drawer next to his pajamas.

Just before dawn, he drops off into crazy dreams. When he opens his eyes to the day, Maureen has left for work and it is time for him to get out of bed, to pack. Essentials, he tells himself; he will take only the essentials. He is going to shower, to shave, to rouse his sleepy senses with hot water and the sharp smell of soap; but on the bathroom mirror Maureen has left him a farewell message, scrawled in lipstick:

> *terrible kisses—*
> *indelible love*

and Harris has to think seriously about where he will go, what he will do—what curious stories he will have to invent— before he discovers that the ineradicable pattern of the kisses is like a birthmark signaling the genesis of love, and that the fever of his body is nothing more and nothing less than the relentless climate of Paradise.

Cats

When Kate woke up in the night and felt the warmth of one of the cats against her legs, she could tell which cat it was by reaching out to touch its fur. Cass was sleek, soft as mink or sheared beaver—coats she had touched once when she had gone with Alice Rand to the Lord & Taylor salon— and he was fine-boned, delicate as the yellowed cat skeleton she remembered from her high school biology classroom of nearly thirty years ago. Tibb, who was younger, was also coarser, and his skeleton was both bigger-boned and more compact—a tougher version of cat-ness than Cass—and it was Tibb who was more likely to want to be playful. Where Cass would nuzzle Kate's hand and shift into a new sleep position, Tibb, often as not, would go over on his back and embrace her wrist with the needles of his claws. Sometimes when the two cats were on the bed, one on either side of her, she would lie in the dark and stroke both of them, marveling at the peculiar sensuality of her life.

*   *   *

Lately, after a long time of keeping to herself, she had begun to get involved with a man. His name was Barry, and she had met him at the county clerk's office in June, when she was renewing her driver's license. He stood just behind her in the short line leading to the counter. When she pushed her old license toward the clerk, the man spoke.

"Same birthday," he said.

For a moment she hadn't realized he was talking to her, and then—because no second voice responded—she turned, looked at him.

"We have the same date of birth," he said. "June fifteenth."

"Yes," she said. She smiled at him—a nervous smile, she imagined, for what sort of answer to his flat statement did the man expect? Isn't it a small world. What a funny coincidence. Did he truly think there was something portentous here? "But probably not the same year."

"Nineteen forty-seven," he said.

She shook her head. "No, not quite."

He looked expectant.

She laughed. "You don't really expect me to tell you that I'm older than you, do you?"

Now he was sheepish. "Of course not," he said.

Then it was her turn to be photographed—she wished they could have reused the old picture; it actually looked like her —and she sat on a wooden bench nearby until the new license came out of the laminating machine. The man—tall, trim mustache, exactly thirty-seven years old—sat next to her on the bench.

"I hate to see what it's going to look like," she said. "The picture."

He cocked his head to look at her. "I shouldn't think you'd have to worry about that," he said.

*   *   *

When he asked her to have lunch, she decided to accept. He
flattered her, he seemed unthreatening, and if he turned out
to be married—well, this was only lunch.

In the restaurant, they sat at a table by a window, where
they were surrounded by hanging planters and overlooked the
river, so slow-moving at this time of year that it held the
shade of the nearest bridge in a perfect inverted arch.

He extended his hand across the table. "Barry Miner," he
said.

She took the hand for a moment—it was warm, dry—and
released it.

"Kate Eastman."

She was nervous then, and that meant she talked too
much. She said far more about herself than she had done, or
had the opportunity to do, in the two years since her divorce.
She confessed that she was older than he was, by five years,
and that she had two grown sons. She told him—brightly,
as if it were something she was by now entirely comfortable
with—how fortunate she was to have married a man
decent enough to stay with her until the boys were sent
through college. She told him she had just started working
as a paralegal in the office of one of her former husband's
friends.

Through all of this he listened intently, never taking his
eyes from her face, and finally she tried to encourage *him* to
talk. "What is it you do?" she said.

"I'm a psychotherapist. In that clinic across from the courthouse."

"Oh, heavens. I'd better watch what I say." And she wondered what she had already let out that might have marked
her in his eyes as a "case."

In the weeks that followed, she became more comfortable
with Barry, less compulsive. She learned all over again—such
a long time since she had forgotten!—that her own silences

could draw a man out, that she did not need to interrogate him. He told her that his mother had recently died of cancer —something he revealed almost apologetically, almost as if the woman had done it because it was popular.

"We all worry about it," Kate said, defending her. "It's a terrible, fearful thing, and women have to deal with it."

He had gone silent then—rebuked, perhaps—and she felt vaguely guilty. That was the first night she went to his apartment, the first time she let him persuade her into bed. Afterward she was flustered by what she had done and woke him long before dawn to tell him that she had to leave, that she couldn't be out all night.

"But you live alone," he said.

"Not exactly," she said. And she told him about Cass and Tibb while she put on her clothes to go home to them.

At first he seemed amused by her fondness for the cats. She realized she had let herself in for a good bit of teasing from him, as if she were an eccentric, tolerable despite her odd behavior.

"Do you talk to them?" he asked her once.

"Certainly," she said. She was in bed with him, the second time—later on she would be chagrined to notice that she could remember each time they went to bed by some curious talk that had passed between them—and he was on one elbow, searching her face for God-knew-what knowledge he thought she was keeping to herself. "Shouldn't I?"

"You don't catch yourself sometimes and feel a little foolish?"

"What for?"

"For talking to animals?"

She pondered, not certain how he expected her to respond. "I'd feel foolish if they answered back," she said. "Is this a real discussion, or are you just filling in the time until you get excited again?"

He laughed then, and hugged her. "I'll have to meet them myself," he said. "The cats."

"They'll think you take the world too seriously."

"I suppose. At least I take you seriously."

"I wonder why. I almost feel as if you're picking me apart."

"I don't know what it is," he said. "I guess it seems to me that women like you live your lives on the edge of your emotions."

"Women like me?"

"Older, living without men." He reached out to touch the wisp of hair that had fallen alongside her right temple. "You're at risk somehow."

"But men without women . . . ?"

"Not the same. Men are more inner-directed."

"You have such piercing blue eyes," Kate said. "I'm glad I'm not one of your clients."

But she was thinking about what he had said, and whether she thought it was true or not. What came immediately to mind was her husband—her ex-husband—and how when he worked on the car, sometimes a bolt would be rusted and immovable, or something would break or get scratched while he was trying to remove it. She remembered how he would come into the kitchen, his hands black with grease and orange with rust, and sit at the kitchen table, putting his head in his dirty hands and sobbing quietly. How she would stroke his hair, try to console him. How finally he would stop crying, and lift his face to her, and she would smile because the grease and rust had made splotchy patterns on his cheeks.

"So am I," he said.

"So are you what?"

"Glad you're not one of my patients."

I should hope so, she thought; all that fuss over talking to pets.

Less than a week later she invited him to her house to spend the weekend. She imagined things were getting "meaningful," that when a woman began to make a habit of a man, "something should come of it"—a statement she dimly recalled hearing from her mother.

"I think he has me at a real disadvantage," she said once in the midst of a conversation with Alice Rand. "I haven't been courted in twenty-five years. I don't remember what's expected of me, let alone what's expected of him."

"There aren't any expectations anymore" was Alice's response—Alice, who had chosen "career" in place of marriage and thought all men were children; who had finished law school and now, nearly fifty years old, was a partner in the firm. "Maybe you should just enjoy your disadvantage," she said.

Still, Kate had expectations she could not define—Barry was so intense with her, so relentlessly attentive. She appreciated the attentiveness. She waited for it to "come to something."

Saturday after dinner he said, "I don't think it's healthy for you to live in this solitary way. It isn't normal."

"How much time does a therapist spend with 'normal' people?" she said.

"You know what I mean." He sighed in what she imagined to be a professional exasperation. "You should have more contact with the world. Maybe you should entertain, play bridge, give a party once in a while."

"I'm a terrible bridge player. I have no card sense."

"Monopoly, then. Trivial Pursuit."

"And I hate giving parties—running around pouring salt on the carpet where the burgundy got spilled, rubbing Vaseline into the piano to get rid of the rings from wet glasses." She poured more coffee. "The cats are sociable enough, and a lot easier to deal with."

He sat back in the chair and looked at her. "Easier than me, I suppose," he said.

"I don't know," she said. How ought she to respond to that wistful expression on his face? "I truly don't."

"Why don't you find out?" he said.

"How?"

"Live with me."

She set the coffeepot back on the stove. Alice was right: Mother would never have expected that; and she gave the proposition—it certainly wasn't yet a proposal—her careful consideration. Would she give up the solitude? Probably. Could she be married again, to someone like Barry? She thought so; she had imagined it often enough. Would she move in with him? She didn't know. She was distracted all evening, and slept badly all night.

At the breakfast table on Sunday, Barry rattled the comics while she cooked bacon and eggs. Domestic bliss. Sunday had always been the one day of the week when she felt most like a woman, when she could wear a frilly robe without feeling overdressed.

Barry cleared his throat. "What was all that racket at three in the morning?" he said.

"It was my fault," she said.

"No, it was those damned cats—on and off the bed, scratching the box springs, meowing in my ear. What was the matter with them?"

"It took me a while to figure out. I kept thinking they wanted to be let out, but every time I got one of them near a door, he bolted back inside. After I'd gotten out of bed three times—" She stopped, the spatula poised above the frying pan. "How do you like the yolks? Runny? Hard? In between?"

"Between."

"After three times I finally got the message. The cat dish was totally empty, not a grain of Cat Chow to be seen. It's the first time they've ever confronted an empty food dish, and it put them in a tizzy."

"I'll bet," he said.

"Once I'd filled the dish—and the water bowl was low, too —they quieted down."

"What time was all this, actually?"

"I think it began around quarter of three, and I didn't solve the problem until four-fifteen or so. Some mother, aren't I?"

He shook his head. Sadly, she thought.

She turned the eggs and brought two plates down from the cupboard. "I've been thinking about what you said. About moving in with you."

"And?"

"And I've been thinking about some of your favorite words. 'Healthy' is one of them, and 'normal.' " She arranged three strips of bacon on each plate. "But they always seem to be applied to things *I* do. How about you?"

"Am I healthy and normal?"

"I mean, how normal is it to be thirty-seven years old and never married?"

He seemed not to have been offended by the question. Instead, the next time he visited her, he was even more serious toward her. He stood at the living-room window, looking out over her three acres with their cedars and plums and spruce, and talked, solemnly and at great length, about women and his life. He was an only child. His father had died when he was three, he had been raised by his mother and his mother's elder sister, and he had never really known male comradeship —a "male role model." He hadn't owned a dog, or turtles or gerbils or a pony—any of the masculine trappings of conventional boyhood. His aunt had a canary, which sang in a brass cage. He remembered his first day of kindergarten: he hadn't even gone into the school building at the boys' entrance, but instead went in with the girls, holding hands with Betty Jean, the daughter of his mother's best friend, who lived next door. Still, he told Kate, he believed he was well adjusted. Did she really believe he ought to have married? Wasn't that what men expected of women, and didn't women despise the expectation?

Kate had no answer to that. Hers was an opposite experience, she told him: three brothers; a he-man father—duck hunter, fisherman, camper—still robust in his early seventies; the attentions of uncles and boy cousins and, in school, plenty of boyfriends. She had married a man her father approved of, had given birth to two boys, had been surrounded all her married life by males—husband, sons, a succession of male dogs, the two cats. Perhaps she'd been out of line with the marriage comment, but Barry could see, couldn't he, how different her life had been.

"You don't have to apologize," he said.

"I'm not," she said. Good Lord, did he think she was?

A week passed. Kate wondered how long she would put off deciding whether or not to live with him, but she convinced herself that she only wanted to give him time to understand her. For one thing, it seemed important that he accept the cats.

"Sometimes when I get up in the morning, only one of them will be at the porch door," she said to Barry. "If it's Cass, I'll give him his breakfast and then let him out again. 'Go find your brother,' I'll say. And sure enough, in five or ten minutes Tibb appears. And vice-versa."

"If Tibb comes home alone, you send him after Cass?"

"Yes."

He sipped her bitter coffee. "I thought they weren't brothers," he said.

"They aren't, really. But they think they are. It can't do any harm if I let them go on thinking so, can it?" She smiled at him. "As a psychologist, what's your opinion?"

"I think it's all coincidence, of course. The other cat just happens to come back shortly after the first has gotten fed. I think it's all right to be silly over animals, so long as you know you're being silly."

"How can it be silly if it pleases me and doesn't hurt anyone else?"

"I said it's okay, if you know you're doing it."

"But you see," she said, "it isn't coincidence. If it only happened once in a while—that would be coincidence. It happens regularly."

He sighed. "If you say so," he said.

"Do you think I'm crazy?" she said. "Or only neurotic?"

Gradually, Barry began to be impatient. She caught him watching her, one eyebrow raised, as if he expected her to blurt out what he wanted to hear. He sat on the edge of the bed after they made love, his hands folded, his head bent in thought. He made her terribly nervous; she wondered if he wanted her to feel guilty. Guilt he could probably cope with.

"I don't mean to press," he said one day. They were having drinks together, in a bar near the courthouse. "But I wish you'd give me an answer. You know how I feel about you."

She thought she did.

"I realize how much you like living on the outskirts," he said. "But think about the conveniences of living in town. Shopping. Closer to your work. The gas you'll save."

"I think about Cass and Tibb."

He looked away, revolved a sweating tumbler between his hands.

"I know you think I'm foolish," she said. "But I couldn't give them up, and I couldn't ask them to be house cats, never able to go outdoors—to hunt, to have all that freedom."

"They could go outside," he said.

"In all the town traffic," she said. "I'd be worried sick. I'd—" She stopped herself, having at that instant an image of one or the other of the cats—they looked so much alike that in the distance of the image she couldn't tell which it was—stiff and dead in a gutter, gold eyes staring, empty. "What might happen," she said. "I can't even think about it."

"And I suppose that means you can't think about living with me." His eyes were averted; his mouth was petulant.

Indirection, she thought. We reach a place without knowing we were headed toward it.

"I'm sorry," she said. "I suppose it does."

He stopped calling her—which was a kindness, Kate thought. At least it was not sex he wanted from her, or not sex only, and for a while she luxuriated in having reclaimed her bed. She imagined the cats were pleased: they were less restless beside her. And she slept better as well—though one morning she woke out of a nightmare in which Cass appeared in the bedroom with a small rabbit squirming in his jaws. Awake, she couldn't decide whether the rabbit was a gift or a warning.

That evening when she fed both cats and let them out, the disturbance of the dream was forgotten. She talked with them as she held the door, saying to Tibb, "Now you be careful," and to Cass, "You take care of Brother, won't you?"

Later she stood at the kitchen window, putting together a salad for her own supper. The cats were moving down the long driveway—Cass in the lead, purposeful, rarely looking back; Tibb following, stopping, then trotting to catch up. Watching them go, she felt a welling-up of emotion she hadn't known since the days when her sons went off to school together.

That's love, she told herself. *There's nothing foolish about love.*

Silent Partners

Lately, Alex sees his rival, whose name is Jennifer, almost every afternoon in the dim corridor, fourth floor, of the new language building. A small young woman, moon-faced and owl-eyed in her round glasses, Jennifer is hanging out, waiting to meet Pauline after class.

Pauline is his ex-wife. Jennifer is her lover. The two women have lived together for nearly a year.

At first Alex blamed himself. Sitting with Pauline in the student cafeteria, overlooking a river dotted with brown ducks, he had tried to understand.

"We rented a place across the river, near the hospital," Pauline told him. "I know you're disgusted. I just thought you ought to know, even if you aren't my husband anymore."

"No, no," he said, "I'm not disgusted. Just surprised."

"Surprise is good. You mustn't ever take things for granted."

"Do I know her?"

"Jennifer," Pauline said. "You saw her once; she stayed behind to help me clean up, the night we gave the election party."

"And you're happy."

She studied him. "I truly am. Probably for the first time since before you and I were married."

"Truly?" He repeated the word as if it were from another language.

"My God," Pauline said, "do you want an affidavit from Jennifer?"

Now, thinking back to his courtship of Pauline, to their meetings when classes were done for the day, he remembers her swagger, overconfident and mannish, as if she carried a chip on her shoulder. He remembers that she smoked cigarettes like a poker player, a factory hand. When he also remembers their times in bed—her passion, her sensitivity to his own desires—he blames her for subterfuge, for sexual deception. Sometimes he admits to himself that he is going out of his way to disown his past with her.

Not to mention his past with other men in her life, before she met him. That fiancé of hers, Timothy. When Pauline and Alex first began making love in her tiny apartment just down the hill from the university, Timothy's photograph hung in plain view on the wall at the foot of the bed.

"Close your eyes," Pauline said when he suggested that she ought to take down the picture. "Don't look at a man when you're loving me."

One day they were driving in the city where the fiancé lived. It is still an uncomfortable memory for Alex.

"Tim's apartment isn't far from here," Pauline had said.

"Terrific."

"I'm not trying to make you jealous," she said. "But it's a nice place. You'd like it."

"Maybe I would," Alex said.

"I happen to know he's out of town."

"Even more terrific."

"And I still have a key."

He marvels now—he marveled then—at her apparent contempt for Tim, a man she was promised to. Yet it was exciting: going there, whispering in the hallway while Pauline unlocked the door, drinking Timothy's whiskey, thrashing in Timothy's bed. Pauline insisted they leave the bed rumpled and unmade, so Tim would know.

Alex wonders if Jennifer guesses how cruel Pauline can be—if she will someday learn, for instance, that not long ago, after they had met by chance at the shopping center downtown, he and Pauline went to the apartment near the hospital and made love. When will Pauline tell her?

Jennifer knows who he is. Pauline has introduced them: "My friend, Jennifer. My once-upon-a-time, Alex." He told Jennifer he was pleased to meet her. Jennifer seemed frightened and shy.

When he was in bed with Pauline, he had said, "What's it like for a woman to make love to a woman?" As soon as he asked, he wished he hadn't.

Pauline avoided the question. "Loving is loving," she said.

"I'm sorry," he said. "It was a dumb thing to ask." He was ashamed to have brought it up.

"It isn't dumb," Pauline said. "It just can't be answered."

Later, when he was putting on his clothes in the bedroom she shared with Jennifer, Alex caught Pauline watching him out of the dresser mirror. "This is my first time with a man in more than a year," she said, not turning to face him. "It wasn't *so* bad."

This Monday afternoon he comes down the west stairwell of the language building on his way to the parking lot, having just taken a German Poetry quiz he knows he has failed. On the third-floor landing a small group of students has come out of a sign-language class, and they are continuing to make silent conversation. Alex has watched them before; he is fascinated by their gestures, by the animation of their faces despite the absence of spoken words, by the apparent ease of their communication. He thinks of how many ways there are for men and women to relate to one another—and in the same thought, What about me?

At the moment he isn't relating to anyone. He is an otherwise normal twenty-nine-year-old man alone in a world of pairs, divorced by a wife he lived with for five years, having no genuine hope of replacing her. His dreams—finishing graduate school, finding a decent job, raising a family—are like so much smoke, swept aside on the winds of sexual freedom. Pauline may continue to be his friend, but not the mother of his children.

While he is feeling sorry for himself, Pauline emerges from the classroom, mingles with the other students, then notices Alex.

"What a surprise," she says.

He hasn't seen her in nearly three weeks; she seems paler, thinner, but the brightness of her eyes does not suggest sadness. "Are you studying that stuff?" he says.

"Yes. For Jennifer. I'm getting pretty good at it."

"For Jennifer?"

Pauline raises an eyebrow. "You didn't know she's deaf?"

"No."

"Since she was eight," Pauline says. "Some weird complication from measles." She considers Alex's look of disbelief. "Can't you imagine two people being happy and quiet at the same time?"

"But she isn't . . . " He stumbles on the word. Pauline has fallen into step alongside him, descending the cement steps that echo harshly under her heels.

"She isn't mute," Pauline says. "She's just not good at talk —like someone with a slight speech impediment. Anyway, I

prefer silence when I'm alone with her. That's why I've been
learning to sign."

"And you're really good at it?"

"Good enough to carry on an argument." As they go out
the back door into the parking lot, she gives him a sly, sidelong glance. "Want to try me?"

"No," he says. He wonders if this isn't a good time to tell
her how lonely he is. "Can I give you a lift?"

"Jennifer's picking me up." Pauline shields her eyes from
the afternoon sun and surveys the parking lot. "There she is."

Alex looks where she is pointing. Jennifer is standing by an
opened car door. She waves. Pauline waves back, and runs to
the car, still waving.

Now when Alex sees Jennifer he feels differently toward her.
Now he is more hopeful of reconciling with Pauline, redraw-
ing his dreams of family and of ordinary success, for perhaps
it is not love she feels for Jennifer after all. Perhaps it is
sympathy, or pity, of the sort sensitive people feel for the
handicapped. Poor Jennifer. She has—what do they call it
now?—a "communicative disorder."

He looks forward to meeting her in the university halls or
on the campus walks. He says "Hello" to her, out loud, pretending still to be unaware of her deafness. Jennifer doesn't
know that Alex is patronizing her, just as she seems not to
know that Pauline has been unfaithful to her, not so very
long ago.

One evening Pauline telephones, weeping, and asks him to
come to the apartment. By the time he arrives, he is a man
who has come courting; he lacks only the bouquet of flowers,
the box of chocolates.

When Pauline opens the door, Alex is shocked. Tonight
her eyes reflect the sleeplessness he had looked for earlier, and

she seems as unhappy as—in his perverse desire for reunion
with her—he has sometimes wished.

"I had to talk to someone," she says. "Jennifer's moved
out."

Alex can't think how to respond.

"I'm going crazy," Pauline says. She motions him to a
chair, and sits on one end of the sofa, across the room from
him.

"What happened?"

She shakes her head. "There was no note or anything. Just
empty bureau drawers, all her clothes gone from the closet.
I've called everyone I can think of who knows her."

Alex sits helplessly. Pauline has never worn much makeup,
but what little she does wear is streaked with tears that have
not quite dried. Her hair is uncombed. She has on a blue
peignoir that shows her thighs. He watches her reach for a
cigarette and light it.

"You asked me once what it was like to love a woman,"
she says.

"It was an improper question. I felt guilty about it for a
week."

"And those were the days when you didn't know about
Jennifer—that she was deaf."

"I just thought she was terribly shy. I imagined she was
afraid of me, or resented me."

"I told you then," Pauline says, "that loving was loving,
and that the object of it didn't really make a difference—but
that wasn't true. It isn't true."

She looks at him through the blue curl of cigarette smoke.
"The delicacy of loving a woman," she says. "The intimate
way we understand ourselves. It's like a welcome peace." She
lays the cigarette in the ashtray and folds her hands in her
lap. "When I made the signs for 'I love you,' I'd make them
very slowly, and I'd feel my heart flutter against the word
'love.' Then sometimes I'd take her fingers and press them
against my throat, and say it out loud: 'I love you.' Letting
her feel the resonance of the words."

Alex looks away. His ex-wife is embarrassing him, he thinks.

"Or I'd put my mouth against her skin—anywhere—and say those words over and over and over. I swear, after a while I could feel her whole body singing with love-words."

"Jesus, Pauline," he says.

Pauline smiles. "I told you: the question wasn't improper. Just difficult." She rubs the heels of her palms against her damp cheeks. "Thank you," she says. "I feel better, talking about it."

"And what now?"

"I don't know. Tell me how to go about winning someone back."

He wants to say something clumsy about how easily *he* could be won back, but he can tell—by her sadness, her tears, the passion of all she has told him—that the time is not right. "Well," he says instead, "I guess you just have to hang in there."

When Alex comes down the west stairwell after class the next day, two women are standing against the light at the third-floor landing. When he has passed and looks back, he sees that one of them is Jennifer. The other is a dark-haired older woman he doesn't recognize. They are deep in the artful conversation of the deaf, and he stops for a moment, two or three steps below the landing, to watch them. It is wonderful: the eloquence of Jennifer's signs, the expressiveness of her gestures. Her lips move slightly, as if she is saying to herself the words she will pass to her partner—giving them a silent rehearsal before turning them over to the easy instrument of her hands. He can almost see why Pauline is attracted to Jennifer. Alex wishes he were able to read these words, to understand the connections women enjoy that shut him out so entirely.

Sisters

"What are you up to?" Karen says. "What do you think you're doing to your face?"

"Nothing," Liz says. Karen is the older sister, married, separated, back home to stay for a while in their mother's house. Liz is fifteen, and feels that it's no business of Karen's what she is doing to her face, though the simple truth is that she is highlighting her cheekbones with blush. The cheekbones are her best feature, or so she has been told. Her next-best feature is her long hair, which she is thinking about having streaked. "I'm going out."

"Is that blush? That purple stuff? You're using too much."

"It's what they call the 'bruised' look," Liz says.

"I know what they call it. It's sick."

"You're too one-way," Liz says. "Too sensitive." Karen's husband, Ty—soon to be her ex-husband—is supposed to have knocked her around; that's why she is home, back in

Elizabeth's room after three years of living with a man. Liz doesn't mind, exactly—she likes Karen—but she feels that the older sister's return is unnatural, like coming back to childhood, and sometimes she resents the loss of her privacy. Now, for instance.

"Not sensitive," Karen says. "Sensible."

"I'm getting ready for a date." She can't tell who with, but thinks she had better say it is Gerald. Karen knows Gerald; she refers to him as "old prunes and prisms," because of the way he holds his mouth when he talks to her. "It's only Gerald," Liz says.

"You're not doing that paint job for Gerald," says Karen.

"Then who for?"

"For anybody. That's the trouble."

"I don't know what that means."

"You're setting traps," Karen says, "and you don't even know what the game is."

"I'm just going to the movies." Liz leans into the mirror to put on her earrings. She has recently had her ears triple-pierced, a decision she sometimes regrets—all those holes to keep open. But she has bought herself three pairs of earrings: emerald, ruby, and diamond—not genuine, of course—that make her feel extravagantly dressed up. "Not to some kind of orgy."

Karen lights a cigarette and sighs smoke in the direction of her sister.

"What time is he picking you up?"

"I'm meeting him at the mall."

"That's tacky," Karen says. "What kind of a man won't even take the trouble to pick his date up at her door?"

"It was my idea; do you mind?" Liz says. "I have an errand to do in the mall, and I told him I'd meet him there." She finishes with the earrings. "Anyway, who the hell are you to give advice about men?"

*　*　*

Later, Karen sits at the kitchen table drinking from a can of beer while her mother rinses the dinner dishes.

"What do you think of Liz's friend Gerald?" Karen says.

Her mother scrapes at a dirty plate and seems to hesitate— weighing the risk of the question, perhaps—before answering.

"I don't object to him, if that's what you're asking," she says.

"You don't think she's awfully young to be going out with him?"

"She's nearly sixteen. Imagine the argument I'd get if I tried to keep her from dating."

"That isn't what I mean."

"Then what?"

"I mean you could suggest she might be a little more careful about who she runs with."

"What do you think is wrong with Gerald?"

"I told you: he's too old for her." And too prissy, Karen is tempted to say; a pink, chinless old lady. But that isn't the point.

Her mother shuts off the faucet and comes to the table. "I suppose he's in his late twenties," she says, sitting across from Karen. "Is that old?"

Karen sets the beer can down with remarkable vehemence. "My God, Mother," she says, "where is your head?"

But she knows where it is; it's thinking about everything except whatever might be difficult to cope with. Karen's divorce, for instance. The divorce is supposed to be final in two more months, but the only thing that upsets her mother is what she refers to as Karen's *attitude*—the word is always emphasized, underscored, in her voice—Karen's criticisms of Liz, which she is afraid sooner or later are going to lead to a quarrel. Karen wishes she could see that her intentions are the best; she doesn't want her little sister to make the same mistake she made when she got married to Ty. Her mother ought to understand; but so far as Mother is concerned, Ty is

just another man with a bad temper. Instead of paying attention to the facts of the marriage, her mother prefers to com-
plain about Karen.

"You're too critical of Little Sister," her mother says. "I
think it's because you coop yourself up in this house all day
long."

"I don't have anyplace I want to go," Karen says.

It's the truth. She spends much of the day in her room—
Liz's room—smoking and reading. Sometimes she helps with
meals; sometimes she offers to do the housework. When the
telephone rings she almost jumps out of her skin. Her mother
cannot seem to imagine what happened in the marriage to
make Karen so frightened.

"It's too bad you and Ty didn't have any children to occupy
your energies," her mother says.

Karen bristles. "I thank God," she says. "I thank God and
Jesus I never gave that man a baby."

But she remembers when she didn't feel like that. Right
after they got married, she would drop in for coffee—while
Ty was at the foundry—and tell her mother how she could
hardly wait to have lots and lots of kids.

When Liz arrives at the mall, Ty is sitting on a bench near
the fishpond. He wears jeans and a Western-style blue shirt
with epaulets and mother-of-pearl buttons; his calfskin boots
have elaborate scrollwork up the sides.

"Hey, sweetie," he says.

"I'm sorry I'm late," Liz says. "I had this long conversation
with your wife."

He blinks at her. He has watery-blue eyes whose gaze never
stops on any single object, as if he is trying to see everything
at once.

"I thought you wasn't coming," he says. "I pitched in all
those pennies, wishing for you."

He gestures toward the fishpond, its bottom covered with

pennies, hundreds of them, along with a sprinkling of nickels and dimes. Half the people in the mall toss pennies into the pond; the mall owners sweep up the coins every couple of months.

"Well," Liz says, "if you've thrown away all your money, I guess you can't afford to take me to the movie."

"I figured you probably seen the movie anyway."

"Why would you figure that?"

Ty stands up and takes her hand. His belt buckle says INDIAN.

"Your hair surely smells good," he says. "Let's walk."

For a while they stroll in the mall, hand in hand. Ty towers over her; there is a swagger about him that Liz likes, and whenever they stop in front of a store window—she likes to look at clothes; he goes for sporting goods and hardware—she squeezes his muscular upper arm and presses her face against the sleeve of his shirt. He smells of tobacco and sweat, makes her feel drugged. By the time he leads her out to the parking lot, Liz is weak from wanting to be kissed and touched.

The pickup is in its usual place, in a dark corner behind the Firestone store that went out of business a few months ago. They sit in the cab and kiss for a long time. Ty's kisses too are tobacco-flavored, and his tongue is coarse in her mouth. Sometimes they stop kissing for a few minutes while Ty smokes a cigarette. One time he had a reefer; he coaxed Liz to take a drag, but she practically strangled on the sweet smoke, and he laughed at her.

When he gets serious and reaches under her dress, Liz has to decide when she will say no to him. She likes what he makes her feel; he knows what to do with his hand there—which is more than she can say for the two or three school-boys she has let touch her—and it is always tempting to let him keep on, to find out what new things will happen to her. What she likes best is to lean her head against his chest, her eyes closed, one foot up on the seat and the other on the floor of the truck while he rubs her with the flat of his hand. She feels helpless and dreamy, as if she is floating, and she wishes Ty could do this to her forever.

"I don't understand why my sister hates you," she says.

"She's cuckoo," he says, "that's why. She's plain cuckoo."

Liz squirms under his hand. "I think she must be," she says, so softly she can scarcely hear herself.

Karen would go to bed if she thought she could sleep, but she knows she can't. Downstairs, in the living room, she sits on the arm of the big chair that used to be her father's, where she can look out the bay window and watch the street in front of the house. Something is fishy. In her stomach she can feel a knot of fear, something like a ball of yarn wound tightly from the skein of her nerves.

It is two in the morning. Little Sister isn't home, and Karen knows she has been lied to. Her mother knows it too, but she went to bed at midnight; lately Mother solves all unpleasantness by going upstairs to bed.

The question is: Who did Liz meet? Karen thinks she knows, and this is why she is afraid. She remembers all the questions Liz used to ask when Karen got home from heavy dates with Ty—Where does he take you? What does he do? Is it fun?—and Liz's eagerness, her childish excitement. She remembers how Ty looked at Liz when she visited the trailer, after the marriage. She remembers things he said: how fast Liz was growing up, how maybe he'd married the wrong sister —trying to make it sound like a joke, but all the time looking at Liz as if she were something to eat. Part of her mind tries to say No, Liz isn't that dumb, Liz knows better, Liz is just dating some greasy-haired rowdy she doesn't want the family to meet—some gas-pump jockey, some high school dropout she's a little ashamed of. But the other part of Karen's mind —the part that imagines the worst because the worst is what makes the world turn—knows, just knows, it's Ty.

She also remembers how attractive Ty can be, his strength, his easiness with girls. And good looks; he certainly has the

looks, and the pale-blue eyes she used to see herself helpless
in. Lost in. Terrified in.

She shivers and leaves the chair, pulls her robe tight about
herself and goes out to the kitchen. She puts a half-spoonful
of instant in a mug, runs the hot-water tap until it steams up
from the stainless sink. The rattle of the spoon as she stirs the
coffee is like a bell, an alarm that keeps going off inside her
head: *Ty, Ty, Ty, Ty, Ty.*

She sits on the window seat with the coffee mug cradled
between her hands. When Ty's pickup appears out front, she
recognizes it, even in the dark, by the crooked cross of strap-
ping tape on the windshield where a pebble cracked the glass.
She watches Liz climb carefully out of the cab, carrying her
blue cardigan, one long sleeve dangling to the ground, and
she thinks: *Ty, you smug bastard, if you've hurt my sister I'll kill
you.*

At first Liz thinks the shadow half-hidden by the living-room
curtains belongs to her mother, which is surprising; but then
she remembers that Karen has moved home and it is Karen in
the window, which is not surprising at all. When Ty's truck
roars away, the shadow disappears. The hall light comes on.
Get off my back, damn it, Liz thinks. She opens the front
door.

"Your so-called 'date' telephoned," says Karen.

"That stupid Gerald," Liz says.

"Do you have any idea what you're asking for?" her sister
says. "Look at yourself. Look at your hair. Look at your
clothes. I suppose he's got your underpants for a souvenir."

"If you're so jealous, why don't you go back to him and be
his wife?"

Liz catches a glimpse of herself in the hall mirror; she does
look like a kind of a mess.

"You don't know what he'll do to you," Karen says. "You
don't know how strong he is."

"I don't want to hear your horror stories," Liz says. "I want to go to bed." She can't deal with this right now—that much she knows. She is still drifting in the pleasure Ty gives her with his hands, still watery in her knees. She doesn't feel like a fight with Karen, who anyway has lost all sense of perspective when it comes to Ty.

"You think they're stories," Karen says.

"I don't know what they are. I just know I'm tired." She has heard all this—overheard it, anyway—when Karen would come home and sit in the kitchen, sobbing, talking in a high, funny voice. She has caught bits and pieces of Karen's stories: swearwords, Ty's name, things she says he's done. She believes the stories and doesn't believe them, both at the same time.

"Look," Karen is saying. She has pulled back the long lock of hair that always covers the right side of her forehead, tipped her face to the light for Liz to see where a long pink scar, tiny marks like sewing-machine stitches showing on both sides of it, runs from her hairline to just in front of her ear. "Look at that, damn it."

"Ty did that? How? How could he have?"

"I'd got back from the laundromat with a basket of wet wash. He'd missed me. He was mad because he couldn't find me."

"He loved you," Liz says.

"So he swung his fist at me and knocked me against the clothesline pole. Then he grabbed the first thing he could get his hands on. He grabbed my wet jeans off the top of the basket and started whipping me across the face." She puts her fingers up to the scar. "That's what the zipper did. The zipper from my own blue jeans."

"I don't feel like talking about it," Liz says. She pushes her way past Karen and runs blindly upstairs. She can't think why she has started crying. Perhaps for the hurt her sister has suffered. Perhaps for herself, because she is going to see Ty over and over again until she knows everything Karen knows.

Guilty Occasions

We're gathered in front of the television set in Larry Beal's living room on Oak Street, the street where Elaine and I used to live. On the screen is a view of the local Catholic church as seen from somewhere behind and to the right of the altar. What we're looking at is the hundred or so men and women —relatives, friends, school chums, Larry's fellow workers at the tractor plant—sitting in polished walnut pews, waiting for Marilou Beal to marry Gerald Grant. The light is terrible. The images are fuzzy. In the background an organ is playing softly, and its pedal tones are distorted by the small speaker of the TV set, so that the music is like something out of a science-fiction movie, haunted and weird. Old women are still being escorted down the aisle on the arms of ushers. The wedding proper is about five minutes away. I know because I was there, this afternoon at a little after three o'clock.

I'm sitting with a glass of Larry's Chivas-rocks in hand, surrounded by Beals and Beal kin, waiting for the replay of

the wedding ceremony. It's nearly eleven at night. The bride
and groom are long gone, and the last batch of people from
the reception at the Sheraton Inn ballroom has just come in
the kitchen door from the driveway. Elaine is at the kitchen
table, laughing with Beverly, who is still in her dusty-pink
mother-of-the-bride dress with the lace hem and the embroi-
dered roses. Every once in a while Elaine looks over at me
and scowls at the glass I'm holding; she's warning me that I'm
the one driving. Little children—I don't know whose they
are, but they appear at every Beal-daughter wedding Elaine
and I have been to, and we've been to them all—are milling
around the living room. Only the flower girl, perhaps three
years old, is settled, quiet in her mother's lap, ready to see
herself on television for the first time in her life. Don't ask
me who the mother is.

Don't ask me who anybody is, actually. I know Larry and
Bev because we lived across the street from them for twelve
years, and I know all the Beal kids—the five girls and the one
boy, Daniel, who ran the video camera—and I recognize
Larry's father and Bev's mother and sister and a few assorted
cousins who show up for these occasions from out of town.
Most of the people in the kitchen and living room tonight I
don't know from Adam.

"That's an awful picture," Larry says. "We're getting a new
picture tube on Monday. We had the TV man out on Thursday and he wanted to take the set right then, but Bev said
no, that would sure leave a terrible hole in the living room
and with a houseful of people coming for the weekend she'd
rather wait."

"You'd have had more room for the houseful of people,"
Larry's father says from the sofa.

"Hell, yes, wouldn't we?" Larry inspects my glass. "You
about ready for a refill?" he says.

"No, thanks," I say.

"Well, you just holler," he says. "You're the only one
drinks that stuff. I keep it in the house just for you."

"I know." Ten years ago Larry and I drank a lot together,

but now he can't drink, and I don't do it much. I'm allergic to it, the truth is.

"The light sure is poor," Larry says, considering the screen.

"It's all that dark wood in the church," Daniel says. "It soaks up the light like you wouldn't believe."

"That's true," his father says. "Soaks it up like a blotter."

As Elaine made clear on the way to the church, I'm fortunate to be here at all. All I'd said, a couple of weeks ago, was that I didn't especially want to go to Marilou's wedding, but as usual it wasn't so much what I said as the way I said it. "I don't like those things," I'd told Elaine. "Weddings and funerals, they're all the same. They depress me."

"You never said that before."

"I never gave it much thought before."

"You don't mean it," she said.

"Yes, I do," I said. "Weddings are depressing, and I don't know any reason to pretend otherwise."

"There's a big difference between a wedding and a funeral," Elaine said. "A huge difference."

"Name it," I told her.

"Weddings are happy. Funerals are sad."

"Phooey," I said. "They're both the end of something."

"Of what?"

"Life as we know it," I said.

That stopped her short. She put her head down and bit her lower lip and worked at unraveling a length of yarn from the needlepoint pattern she's been working for about five months now. I didn't say anything more. This was two Saturdays prior to the wedding, and I was watching football with the sound off, trying to keep track of the action without interfering with anybody else's privacy.

"I guess you'd better stay home from the ceremony," Elaine said then. "You'll jinx it."

"Jinx it?" I said. "How so?"

"If you think it's no different from a funeral," she said.

"You're not serious," I said.

"Yes, I am."

"That's ridiculous. Of course I'm going."

"You'll be bad luck," she said. "You'll be a cloud over the happy couple."

She really seemed to mean it. I had to sit back and think about it—about whether I was going to get Marilou Beal and her beau off to a gloomy start in their wedded life.

"I *have* to go," I said. "What are Larry and Beverly going to say if I don't show up for this wedding, after I've made it to all the others? And what about Marilou? She was always my favorite. How are you going to explain my not being there?"

"I'll say you had to work. I'll say Tim Merriman called early in the morning and needed you to drive to Rochester for him." She never once looked at me. Just plugged away at that needlepoint like it was the center of everything. "They'd never know the difference."

"I'd know," I said. "And you'd know."

"How can you do something you don't believe in?" she asked me. She'd raised her head up from her yarn and was looking me straight on. "How can you?"

"Aren't I married to you?" I said. "Thirty-whatever years, day in, day out?"

Larry Beal has five daughters, and Marilou is the youngest. Five weddings in seven years; that's what Larry and Bev have been doing with themselves in this semi-retirement of his: getting their daughters married off. I knew them all, and I remember all their weddings, and even though it's Elaine's department I know every gift we sent, because we always send the same thing: a set of sterling-silver napkin rings. It's a tradition.

Jane Louise was the first bride, though she wasn't the oldest daughter; she got married to a boy named Bryce, who drove for a private ambulance company in town. It was the second time in my life I'd been inside a Catholic church, and I suppose I spent more time craning my neck to look at the paintings put up along both outside aisles and gawking up at the ceiling-high mosaic of Christ on the Cross behind the altar than I did taking in the ceremony.

That was the first Chivas occasion, the Jane Louise reception, and I was touched by it—Larry and I'd had a sort of falling-out over a dog I sold him just before we moved to the country, and even though the wives continued to be the best of friends, things were touchy between the two of us. There was nothing wrong with the dog, one of the prettiest retrievers I'd ever raised, except that he was gun-shy, and nothing Larry did in the way of training ever changed that. In fact, it got worse; all Larry had to do was unlock his gun rack and the dog would disappear under the nearest bed. Old Larry found the whole business infuriating, and of course I wasn't about to take the dog back. Anyway, the Chivas, which he knew was my favorite even though I didn't often buy it for myself, seemed to say that he wanted to be friends again. "I'm a bourbon man myself," he told me that evening, after Janie Louise and Bryce had left, "and I can't abide Scotch. But I know it's your favorite, and I want you to remember that it's yours any time you want to stop by for a drink."

He meant it. He'd bought a whole half-gallon that sat in its own fancy wood cradle so you could pour it without having to lift it, and I'm sure I'm the only person who's drunk it all these years; it's still nearly half full, and Larry's got no more daughters to celebrate.

Around midnight that first time, when even most of the Beal relatives had gone off to bed, Larry and I sat drinking in his basement rumpus room, and eventually the talk got around to the retriever.

"I never did understand that dog from day one," Larry said to me. "I didn't know if you'd sold me a dog or a goddamned hairdresser."

"They don't have to be frothing at the mouth to be a good bird dog," I said. "They can be gentle and good with kids, and still do you right in the field."

"That dog was so gentle he used to pee when he heard a door slam," Larry said.

"Probably you shouldn't have made a house dog out of him. That didn't help matters."

"The day he got killed by the car—right out there in front of the house—I said to Bev that I figured he'd done it on purpose: threw himself in front of that old lady's Pontiac out of pure shame."

And that was the last anyone ever said about the dog. At future weddings, the chief topic of conversation always came down to what the new people had done to the house across the street where Elaine and I used to live. The new people were always different: one set of them put up a carport, and the next set tore it down and built a two-car garage, and another set got tired of painting and called in some fly-by-night outfit to nail on puke-colored vinyl siding. It was a fact: after we moved out, the neighborhood was never the same, never as settled and comfortable. Sometimes Elaine and I sit in the new house and look out the picture window that gives us the view of the country-club golf course—nobody can ever build there, and that's why we bought where we did and we reminisce about the old place. It was the first house we owned, it was where our two boys did most of their growing up, it was the time when we were young and every day was an adventure. But then we always remind ourselves of what wave after wave of new people did to wreck that house, that neighborhood, and we consider ourselves lucky we moved away.

After Jane Louise it was Suzanne, the oldest girl, who had the big church wedding. I could never figure out where she met the guy, but he was a pip—a fast-talking type from Chicago, whose old man was in real estate—and the happy bride and groom drove to the airport in Hubby's silver Jaguar, then got on Daddy's corporate jet for a flight to the Caribbean.

Neither one of them's been seen at the old homestead since, but Bev always has postcards to show us from the world's far corners.

"Listen to this," she'll say. " 'You and Daddy really have got to see the Taj by night. It's spectacular.' " She'll beam at Elaine. "Isn't that exciting? Don't you envy them both?"

I just look at Larry and roll my eyes, and he puts on this secret smile of his, as if he can read between the lines of the postcard and knows his Suzanne is actually concerned with better things.

Most recently the weddings of the Beal daughters have become an annual event. Two years ago it was number three, Candace, who married a college boy majoring in business and accounting, and who went to work two days after the wedding to support him through his M.B.A. Last year it was Jennifer Lynn; she married the gangster—a youngish man with five-o'clock shadow, who wore a black tux with a black shirt and white bow tie, and stood in the reception line with both hands in his trouser pockets so that all he could do was nod his head to the well-wishers. "He's a real spook," Elaine whispered to me. This was at the formal reception—the first one at the Sheraton and the first one immortalized by Larry's new videotape camera—and the groom had got Jennifer off at a table in the corner, from which trap he wouldn't let her out. He wouldn't dance, he wouldn't mingle, and he wouldn't take his hands out of his pockets. "I think his suspenders must be broken," I told Elaine. She nudged me with her elbow. "Don't be awful," she said.

This year: Marilou.

You have to keep in mind that we know the Beal girls almost as well as we know our own kids, and that because Elaine and I brought up two sons, we had a tendency to think of the Beal girls as the daughters we never had. We watched them grow up. In most cases—Janie Louise is the only excep-

tion—we got our first look at them in the hospital the day
after they were born. Our boys used to baby-sit for them; if
Larry and Bev were tied up, Elaine or I would drive them to
tap-dancing class or piano lessons or even catechism on Saturday mornings. We got to consult with the Beals on when
the girls ought to start dating, and to help size up their first
boyfriends. There was even a time when we hoped our Billy
would be the one to get married to Marilou.

There wasn't one Beal wedding that didn't make me con-
jure up some years-back image of the bride. Here'd be Susie,
kneeling at the left of the altar under a statue of the Virgin
Mary, head bowed while the priest said his prayers to God
and the rest of us, and I'd see this little blonde girl with
scraped knees, sitting on the wall below my front porch,
playing jacks. Or I'd be standing with the rest of the company, twisted around to watch Candy marching down the
aisle on Larry's arm, her eyes mostly downcast but lifting
every few steps to take a quick look left or right, finding a
friend or an uncle, and I'd have this flash of a twelve-year-old
kid with braces, standing at my door with an order form for
Girl Scout cookies, trying not to show all that metal in her
mouth.

It's eerie, that kind of double image. When it happens, I
don't feel old, exactly, but I know I'm thinking about time in
a way that's different from the usual. There's a moment that
comes after a wedding, when you're sitting in the hotel ballroom over this terrible combination of a glass of Scotch-rocks
and a piece of sicky-sweet white cake, and a small stir like a
wind sweeps across the assembled guests. It means the bride
and groom are leaving, and when you look up to see them
moving away from you—out the wide doorway, down the
hotel corridor—and vanishing into the elevator, you feel it
again. Time. It's real. It goes on, out doors, along hallways,
up to the penthouse and down to the lobby, whether you're
with it or not.

That's what I feel at the weddings of the Beal daughters,

and it's stronger and stronger with each young woman that used to be a neighbor child of mine.

It's true that Marilou Beal was my favorite from day one. She was born on a chilly Saturday in October, almost exactly twenty years ago, and it was me that drove her mother to the hospital. Larry was off duck-hunting with his father and Daniel, who was then maybe eleven or twelve years old. I'd heard the three of them hitching up the trailer with the old khaki-colored boat at around four A.M.—you know how voices carry at that hour, loud and clear, like sounds over water—and I don't suppose they'd been gone more than an hour when our phone rang. Elaine got up and went into the hallway to answer, and in a couple of minutes she was back, sitting on the edge of the bed and shaking me by the shoulder.

"It's Beverly," she said. "She needs a ride to the hospital. Larry's gone up to the lodge and won't be back till tomorrow night."

"Is it the real thing?" I said.

Elaine punched me. "Get up and get dressed. I'll go over to see if she needs anything packed; you tell Ned he's to be sure that his brother eats some breakfast."

Ned was ten; Billy was five. I got dressed and woke up Ned to tell him what was going on, and by the time I went across the street, Beverly was sitting in the kitchen drinking coffee with Elaine. A small blue suitcase was sitting between the stove and the refrigerator, with a bright blue raincoat draped over it and a couple of thick paperback books perched on top of that.

"I'm all set," Bev told me. "Ready and able."

"How about that Larry," I said. "What timing."

"It's been worse," she said. "When Janie was born, he wasn't even in the country." Korea, she meant.

I carried the suitcase and the books, and Elaine got her into the coat and helped her out to the car. I had a white Rambler wagon in those days, the back end of it always filled with engine parts, and I remember the sound of metal scraping metal all the way to the hospital. I kept apologizing for the racket, but Bev didn't appear to notice. She seemed gloomy; I wondered if she was afraid.

We made small talk. I kidded her some more about Larry picking this day to go hunting, and she kidded me about my asking if she was sure, after five kids, that she was really going into labor.

"Actually," I said, "what I wondered was if you were really sure you were pregnant." I looked over to see if that would make her smile. It didn't.

"This is the last time," she said. "This is the one I didn't want."

I waited around for an hour or so. It was a big hospital, with nuns and nurses and serious young men zooming back and forth, and I wanted to make sure they got her into a bed and that her doctor showed up to see if everything was O.K. I sat for a while in the main waiting room and thought about Bev's not wanting the baby. How could she not? It's the truth that I joshed Larry about all his girls, but he could see I envied him. A couple of years after Bill was born, when Elaine said she thought maybe we ought to talk about having one more baby, I'd asked her straight off if she could guarantee a girl.

"You know I can't," she said.

"Then count me out." It was dumb and cruel to say such a thing, but I'd said it and I couldn't unsay it.

So Marilou was special. She arrived just after noon that day, and in the evening Elaine and the boys and I drove over to St. Francis and peered through the glass at Marilou Agnes Beal, aged six and a half hours, and we looked in on Bev to see that she was all right. Larry still didn't know he had a fifth daughter; I suppose until he found out, Sunday evening, I felt as if it was me who was the father of this beautiful girl baby.

And she was beautiful at every stage of her growing up. By the time she was in first grade, her eyes had turned deep brown and her hair was long and dark and she was one of those tall, leggy little girls who go through the world as if they owned it. She had a tendency to be independent, but she always seemed to know if she'd gone too far; she'd break out in a grin that showed the missing front teeth, and that meant she was sorry for pushing and hoped she could be forgiven.

No matter what age she was, I thought of her as older. It was as if I could always see the woman in her—in a gesture of her hands, a look, the way she carried herself, the words she used. Being the youngest child, she could have had all the company and attention she wanted, and yet it seemed to me she was more of a loner than any of the other Beal girls. I'd see her in the summer in her front yard, a linen napkin spread on the lawn for a tablecloth, two place settings with silverware and plates and teacups laid for herself and one favorite doll. In winter, on gray afternoons, she'd trudge up the Oak Street hill by herself, hauling a sled behind her; I'd watch her run and belly-flop and slide down to the bottom of the street, then pick herself up and trudge back to the top. If Elaine and I were having a drink with the Beals, sitting on their screened porch in warm weather or in their kitchen in cold, I always felt somehow tuned in to Marilou. If she was at home, I could sense it and feel happy; if she wasn't, I felt a peculiar hollowness in myself, a loss. Either way, she was a constant distraction to me.

She was Elaine's favorite as well as mine. As Marilou got older, grew into her teens and became one of these modern girls who look sixteen going on thirty, she spent more and more time with my wife. The two of them shopped together, did sewing together, went to movies together. The first time Marilou ever went to a big city, she went with Elaine, and the two of them stayed at a hotel for three days like sisters out for fun. By then, we'd moved to the country; we saw less of

Larry and Bev, but just as much of Marilou. She'd learned to use makeup, she'd gotten conscious of clothes, she'd filled out to be a real woman. Of course I noticed everything.

One afternoon she drove out to see Elaine without calling first. I heard the dogs out back start up their barking, and when I went to the door, there she stood. She was tall, almost as tall as me, and lovely in the way the young are fitted to loveliness, and she held herself with more confidence than you'd give a seventeen-year-old credit for. I went dizzy from that unexpected vision of her. Desire; pure desire is what I felt. I don't know how else to describe it, except that it was like not having any bones, so that instead of a skeleton holding me upright, it was only the blood pounding through veins and arteries that kept me from falling over.

I didn't do anything, and I didn't say anything except that Elaine wasn't home, but Marilou seemed as flustered as I was. I wondered then—I wonder now—if she'd added it all up: the years of my noticing and admiring her, my being alone in the house, whatever else she might have imagined of me. We smiled and stammered and sort of bowed to each other; she waved when she drove off in her little yellow Toyota. I felt hot and ashamed—as if something had happened that I wouldn't like anybody ever to find out about.

The wedding has started. Larry drifts in with a can of diet soda in his hand. Bev stops talking and leans forward to get a better view of the television screen, Elaine turns to watch the picture. The woman I don't know nudges her flower-girl daughter, but the child is asleep and won't wake up. "She'll be mad at me in the morning," the mother says. "Do you think I ought to pinch her?"

It's crazy, sitting here to watch for the second time a ceremony I nearly didn't go to in the first place. The camera is stationary, so Marilou doesn't get into the picture until she's already let go of her father's arm and is meeting young Gerald

before the altar—and for a moment or two she's blocked by
this suitable man she's marrying. Then the picture gets closer.
Daniel has finished his ushering duties, and he's arrived to
zoom the camera in on his sister; when the couple moves on
to the altar, the camera follows them. The picture is muddy,
broken by streaks and blips of light, and the words the priest
speaks are muffled, as if we're hearing someone talking in
another room. I sip my Scotch and look around. Everyone is
wrapped up in the wedding.

I watch it all. The kneeling and standing and kneeling
again, Marilou's trip to the side altar under the figure of the
Virgin, the exchanging of rings, the priest's blessings on
them. The bridal party takes Communion; most of the guests
line up to follow. When the bride and groom turn away from
the altar the picture suddenly flickers and breaks into a black
frame filled with dancing snow. Then, instantly, we are in
the vestry at one end of the receiving line, the camera hand-
held and jiggling from face to face, greeting to greeting. Here
are the sisters in pastel gowns, the in-laws and relatives, the
friends, the co-workers. Here is Elaine, teary-eyed with the
happiness of the day, hugging Beverly, Beverly laughing as if
she's never had a gloomy day in her life, and Larry, over his
wife's shoulder, proud and loud.

And here I am. The camera follows me until I'm in front
of the bride, taking Marilou's hand, stammering my best
wishes for her happy life. I lean to kiss the bride on the mouth
—but just at that moment she turns her face away so abruptly
that my chin bumps her cheek and my lips barely brush the
dark hair below her bridal cap. I don't even get to kiss her.

In the vestry, when that actually happened, I backed away
and felt stupid and clumsy and ashamed. Tonight Larry gives
me a locker-room punch on the shoulder as he walks past to
wind the tape back, and Beverly catches my eye and gives me
a funny little smile.

"It's a great age, isn't it?" she says. "We can get together
and watch Marilou be married over and over again, just as
often as we want."

Payment in Kind

That summer she had the habit of getting up at first light, dressing quietly in the bathroom so she would not wake her husband, Paul, and going out to the kitchen to make coffee. Sometimes she used supermarket coffee, and once in a while, if the morning seemed in some indefinable way "special," she would take from the cupboard under the sink the small Braun grinder her daughter, Sarah, had given her and fill it with Colombian beans she bought at a specialty shop in Waterloo. The beans were small and dark and slippery; they reminded her a little of the Mexican jumping beans her father had bought for her to hold when she was a child, when she had been distressed to learn that the beans jumped because the warmth of her palms roused a tiny worm—some sort of borer—inside.

It took only seconds to turn the coffee beans to powder. She held the contraption in both hands, her right thumb pressed against its orange button until the hum of the motor rose to a higher, freer pitch. When she unscrewed the plastic top and tipped the grinder over the percolator basket, the coffee that spilled out was fine and deep brown—almost as dark as the Iowa earth—and moist, so that she had to hit the machine a couple of times against the heel of her palm to loosen it.

Then, while the coffee made in the old percolator, she went out to the front porch to assess the day. This summer, morning after morning, the days had been identical: a lip of yellow-orange along the eastern horizon, over which the light streamed into a bowl of sky that looked leaden but would turn out to be a pale, high blue; the air still, seeming, when she breathed, already to carry nearly enough of the weight of heat to smother her; ragged veils of fog hanging in the shallows of the fields that opened away from the farmhouse. And the mornings were not quite silent. The chorus of crickets was constant; there was almost always a solitary robin chirping in one of the ash trees; from the highway a mile to the north she could hear the hollow roar of trailer trucks. Somewhere she had read that in silence, absolute silence, you could hear a high-pitched sound that was your own nervous system, and a deep, boiling sound that was the circulation of your blood. Then the crickets might be her nerves, and the far-off trucks her blood. She didn't know about the robin: something of the spirit, perhaps, that the scientists always left out.

By the time Paul came into the kitchen—at six or seven, depending on what he planned to do with his day—the coffee would be half gone, and he would find her sitting at the table, cup in hand, staring idly out the screen door. He said nothing —he was a man of rare words; in all these years she still could not claim to know him—but took a mug from the drainboard and poured an inch of coffee from the percolator. If his first sip told him it was a store brand, he filled the mug and sat opposite her—not like a man making himself comfortable with his wife, but on the edge of the chair, tensed to go about some unannounced business. If the coffee was the Colombian, he would mutter something just below her hearing and empty the stuff into the sink. Either way, his next move was outside, to the weather station he had put together beyond the shed: rain and wind gauges, tools for measuring temperatures and pressures and moistures—instruments acquired as a hobby, but consulted this year with a regularity bordering on the fanatic. No rain had fallen for six weeks; the heat rose into the nineties or hundreds, day after sweltering day; humidities were high, the barometric pressure high, the winds sluggish. There were not even thunderstorms. After ten minutes with his gauges Paul would come in, scowling. "Better close up the house," he said. Never more words than those, and her heart ached for him.

This morning in mid-August she watched him come back from the ritual of reading the weather and realized, as if for the first time, how old he had gotten—or tired, or whatever it was that happened to a man in thirty years of a working life. His movements showed none of the foolish energy that used to carry him like a caprice of wind from one chore to another, one outbuilding to another, one dream to another. He walked with his head down, his shoulders slouched, one hand tucked into a pocket of his overalls and the other rubbing absently at the back of his neck. When he came up the porch steps and through the screen door, his sigh was audible, a distress signal.

"Better close up the house."

She had heard the forecast on the television news last night: no relief, no rain, highs close to a hundred. In the southern part of the state the government was letting the farmers turn livestock onto their set-aside land early, and some counties were already eligible for disaster loans. She could not recall such a summer.

Paul stood in the middle of the kitchen. He looked as if he were trying to remember something, as if he had been on his way to a place, a task, and was disturbed to find himself in an unexpected setting. Then he turned toward the sink, took a tumbler down from the cupboard and filled it with tap water. He studied the water before he drank it. Dear God, she thought, now is he fretting about the well?

"What is it?" she said.

He drained the glass before he responded, and when he did look at her he compressed his lips in what she took to be an ironic smile.

"I was thinking how my old man could have taken a look at the sky, and at the weathervane on the old barn," he said, "and known just as much about the damned weather as I do by reading all those dials."

"Oh, dear," she said. "Is this going to be the speech against progress?"

"Something like that."

"Take a few minutes and have coffee with me," she said. "You can spare me that."

He pulled out his chair and brushed the orange cat off the seat.

"I'll sit," he said, "but I'll pass on the coffee." He studied her. "What's on the docket this morning?"

"I'm going to can tomatoes—such as they are. Then I'm going into town with Nancy Riker."

Paul heard this information without reacting, his thoughts already somewhere else, his eyes reading linoleum patterns off the floor. She drank her coffee; it was lukewarm and slightly bitter.

"I think I'm going to go into that west forty," Paul said. "I walked through it yesterday. Looks to me like it might make twenty percent, but no more."

"You're going to chop it for silage?"

He nodded. "Burt Stone can feed it to his damned cattle." He hauled himself to his feet. "While you're in town, get me a six-pack of something."

*   *   *

Most of the morning she spent dealing with the tomatoes. The drought hadn't done them any good; there were plenty of them, but they were small and hard, not anything she would have wanted to serve in a salad. It was hot work; by ten o'clock the thermometer outside the kitchen window had reached 89—and that was in shade.

She was interrupted only once—by a woman in a gold Cadillac, who rolled into the yard in a cloud of white dust and came to the back door to talk to her about Jehovah's Witnesses.

In the middle of the serious question of Salvation, Helen cut the woman short. "It's a personal matter, isn't it?" she said. "And I've got tomatoes waiting."

The woman went away. It was only when the Cadillac turned out of the yard that Helen noticed a man slouched in the passenger seat. Perhaps the woman's husband, or father; he had an old face and wore a Panama hat. She thought how she hadn't seen a Panama hat in years and years.

A thick cloud of dust followed the car down the road. All over Iowa these gravel roads were like boundaries, defining the size and shape of the farm fields. Every mile, a road to market—east—west, north—south, and heaven help the ignoramus who wanted to build a diagonal. West forty—that's where Paul was chopping down a cornfield that might have delivered 170 bushels an acre, but wouldn't touch thirty-five because of the weather.

Probably she ought to have said to the Jehovah's Witness lady that she didn't believe in God anyway—that she used to believe, but in the years of living on this farm with Paul she had come to see how everything was up to her and to him, how between them each spring they made something appear from nothing just like any magic, any religious power, and how they controlled the earth and manipulated growing things and almost but not quite used the weather to best advantage. She ought to have told her that the roads and fences were what imposed order on chaos. She ought to have said that eternity was only a succession of growing seasons, and if that were not argument enough she could have talked about Sarah and about Peter and about the third child who never got named because he was stillborn. That might have been the last glimmer of her faith; yes, probably it was. And she ought to have explained to the Jehovah's Witness lady about sweat and machinery and bank loans, and what did God know about all that?

Helen waited until after twelve-thirty to have lunch, hoping Paul would join her even while she knew he wouldn't. She sat at the table in the kitchen, a glass of iced tea and a bowl of bran flakes with milk in front of her, listening to the simmer of the tomatoes on the stove. How much she had gotten used to being alone; now that Sarah and Peter were gone, her life seemed almost reclusive, her marriage like the ritual passage of a man and woman on tracks that paralleled but rarely crossed.

Yet this was to have been the year for her and Paul to rediscover each other. When the Agriculture people announced in the spring that farmers could set aside as much as eighty percent of their land and be paid with surplus grains already stored, it had seemed to Helen that for the first time ever her husband would find time heavy on his hands. All the wives shared that belief. Helen remembered an evening in this very kitchen, in March, when Paul and Burton Stone and Jess Eriksen and Harvey Riker had sat playing a card game called pepper and talked about PIK—Payment-in-Kind—while she and the other wives sewed in the side parlor.

"It'll be like going back to the prairies," Stone had said. "Like the Iowa I knew when I was a kid."

"The hell," Paul said. "The Iowa you knew as a kid was leather jackets and switchblades. What's all this 'prairies' crap?"

Stone grinned. He was scarcely thirty years old, had come home from Vietnam to raise cattle on his father's land.

"You know what I mean," he said.

"Sure do," Riker said. "There won't be nothing growing on half my acres this year."

"Not going to plant cover?"

"Weeds cover." He filled his glass from a new bottle of beer; the foam spilled down the sides and puddled on the tabletop. "If I had horses, I'd plant brome or timothy—maybe alfalfa. But I don't." He lifted the glass and with the side of his palm brushed the spilled beer onto the floor.

"You could do worse than get into the horse business," Jess Eriksen said. "That parimutuel bill's going through. There'll be racetracks all over."

"You could raise greyhounds," Paul said. "They're legalizing dog tracks too."

"They make it legal to race Herefords," Stone said, "I'll be sitting pretty."

"Paul here ought to open a bicycle shop," Riker said. "Now the county supervisors have given the old railroad right-of-way to the bike people, there'd be lots of business real close by."

Paul made a show of looking at his cards one by one. "Play the damned game," he said, refusing to be baited.

Much later, when the pepper was finished and the men had gone home through the crisp night, Helen lay beside Paul in bed and thought about the spring planting.

"I suppose it might be all right," she said. "Letting things go a little way back to nature."

"Don't get all romantic," Paul said. "It's just for this year; nobody's inviting the Indians back to chase buffalo."

"Maybe we could do more things together."

He raised himself on one elbow. "You think I ought to sign up for this PIK program?"

"Weren't you planning to?"

"I might." He lay back. "I might set aside that northeast corner where I need to put in tile; I'd probably have the time —and Harve might want to do the tiling on his side."

"You should talk to him about it," she said. Of course he would find a way to avoid leisure; that was Paul.

He had chuckled then. "That Kraut s.o.b.," he said, "giving me grief about that damned bicycle trail. He knows how I feel. He knows the railroad people promised to give me back the right-of-way if they ever closed down the line."

Finally, she rinsed her dishes and left them in the sink. It was time to pick up Nancy Riker; Paul could make himself a sandwich when he felt like it—if he ever decided to come back to the house before dark.

The Shed was a small white-clapboard place on the outskirts of town. It was a man's restaurant—local farmers, truckers passing through—but the two women stopped in for coffee on the way home from the shopping mall. At the largest of the chrome-and-Formica tables, men in overalls were talking and joking. The men's conversation was not steady; long periods of silence intervened, so that what was said made a pattern of loudness and silence—a rhythm appropriate to custom and long friendships.

Neither Nancy nor Helen had bought much. Helen had rummaged through the remnants in a fabric shop until she found a length of cotton she might make into a summer shirt for Paul, and she had stopped off at Hy-Vee to buy his six-pack of Old Milwaukee. Nancy had bought nothing—had seemed to fall further and further into depression as she followed Helen past the rows of stores in the mall. She was a year or two younger, a small, solemn-eyed woman whose black hair was shot through with gray and whose skin was so pale as to seem translucent. Now she sat across from Helen, digging through her purse until she found a cigarette package with two cigarettes left. She offered one to Helen.

"No," Helen said. "Thank you." She had not smoked in nearly ten years; she didn't propose to start again.

"I don't know why that shopping mall upsets me," Nancy said. She lit the cigarette, then immediately set it to smolder in the ashtray.

"At least it was cool."

"I think it's something to do with all those children—those teeny-boppers, or whatever they call them now. How can they bear to—to just wander like that?"

"I suppose it's that they're young," Helen said.

The coffee arrived. She poured a little sugar into her spoon and stirred it into the cup.

"Do you think they look forward to anything?"

"I certainly hope so." She smiled at Nancy. Am I reassuring? she thought. "Doesn't everybody?"

"I wonder. Sometimes, evenings, I drive the highway into Waterloo, and I see those thirteen- and fourteen-year-old girls standing at the corners, leaning against the traffic-light poles. I swear—I almost know how they feel. Waiting for something. Not really knowing if they'll recognize it when it arrives."

"I think it's always a boy with a car," Helen said.

"And what scares me," Nancy said, "is maybe they're more like us than we give them credit for."

"No," Helen said. "For us it was a boy with a tractor."

"Isn't that the truth?" She stubbed out the unsmoked cigarette. "Do you ever try to imagine what life would be like if you hadn't married a farmer?"

"No. Not since the first two or three years."

"I do," Nancy said. "Dear God, I do."

Helen waited, but Nancy only looked down at the coffee cup cradled in her palms and shook her head.

"I've thought about being married to a different kind of farmer," Helen said. "I've thought: What if we kept hogs?"

She saw the shiver in Nancy's shoulders, hoping the movement meant laughter.

"Oh, Helen." Nancy raised her head. The barest trace of tears glistened at the corners of her eyes, but she was giggling. "Hogs, Helen. The smell, the dirt, the awful noises they make. And they eat people."

"Hog heaven," Helen said.

"Living high off the hogs," Nancy said. She got a handker-
chief out of her purse and dabbed at her eyes. "Hog city." She
subsided. "I'm sorry," she said. "You're such a funny person
when you want to be."

"And sometimes I do want to be," Helen said. She glanced
around the café. The men were still self-absorbed; the waitress
was at the cash register, sorting through meal checks. "You
have to be able to laugh at yourself—it's such a crazy way to
live."

"This is the worst yet."

"I know. You can't think life is all strawberries and cream
with Paul and me."

"I don't even get a civil sentence out of Harvey. I lie awake
these hot nights and I think I'd rather be anywhere else, doing
anything else. Anything."

"Years and years ago, when Sarah and Peter were both
nutty about riding, I did use to think Paul and I could have
made a good thing out of raising horses. The war in Vietnam
was still on. Sarah had that wonderful quarter horse Paul
picked up at the sale barn in Waverly, and Peter talked us
into buying him that huge gelding, Lopez, that was part quarter and part Thoroughbred. Sixteen and a half hands. I
thought we'd have to carry a stepladder so Peter could get up
on him." She smiled, remembering. Why did the very
thought of horses make her sentimental? "Peter was ten or
eleven, I can't think which."

"Sarah stayed with horses a long time," Nancy said.

"She had a year of college left when she finally decided she
couldn't keep up with it, couldn't really give Cloud the care
and the exercise."

"I'd forgotten what she called it."

"Red Cloud. He was a chestnut gelding." She picked up
the check and looked at the numbers. "Sometimes I wish
we'd gone into the horse business. The weather wouldn't
affect us quite so much—I mean, it would affect feed prices,
but it couldn't wipe us out."

"There's other things," Nancy said. "Like in Texas a few years back. Equine something. You recall they used to have that margarine commercial on the television, about not trying to fool Mother Nature? That's what's wrong with marrying a farmer, and it doesn't matter if you raise corn or beans or pigs or horses. You can't fool Mother Nature, but it's okay for Mother Nature to fool you."

"Why not let me buy the coffee?" Helen said.

In the pickup on the way home, they sang Girl Scout songs, and when Helen pulled into the Riker farmyard, Nancy reached out to give her a sweaty hug.

"You're always good for me," she told Helen. "You're the nicest person I know."

Just in the time since she had been at the mall, a portable sign had appeared in front of the Eriksens' produce stand:

SORRY
CLOSED FOR THE SEASON
THANK YOU
GARDEN DRIED UP

The stand was shuttered tight; the fields beyond the Eriksen house and barn and toolshed were either brown or bare. She should tell Paul. He would shrug, look off into that space where he could not be followed.

She turned off the blacktop onto the county road. Inside the fences the fields of corn were brown, straggly, worthless. Only the ditches showed anything growing, and even the green weeds were faded under a thick coating of dust. Nancy's misery was commonplace; they all felt it: what sort of life was it, that you could be fifty years old, a good mother, a patient wife, a strong worker, yet you had no more money, or leisure, or happiness than the day you chose the risk of marriage? Even the mailbox mocked her—its support made from an old

plowshare painted vivid red, and the box in the shape of a
barn with TOBLER printed on its sides as if the display of her
husband's name were no different from a billboard for Mail
Pouch tobacco.

She stopped at the box. A pleasure-horse magazine she had
never had the heart to cancel, even after Peter left home. A
letter from her mother addressed in the failing hand that sent
a chill of fear through her—if she let herself think about it.
Paul's *Farm Journal*. She laid everything on the seat beside
her.

Driving up the narrow lane to the house, she saw that the
farmyard was crowded with young people on bicycles—perhaps a dozen of them, all on the flimsy "English" bikes of her
childhood, fenderless, with hand brakes and skinny tires, the
curious loop of chain at the rear axle, the high, pointed saddle
seats that always looked too uncomfortable to be sat on. Some
of the bikers wore white helmets that perched on top of their
heads and strapped under their chins to make them look like
hockey players or TV roller-skaters. Boys or girls, they wore
cut-offs that showed off their lanky, tanned legs, and sneakers
without socks or colorful biking shoes with knee stockings;
some of them had on T-shirts with slogans: "SCRAMBLED EGGS
AND BEER—NOT JUST FOR BREAKFAST ANYMORE" or "BIKERS
ARE BETTER LOVERS." The women had blonde hair streaked
from too much sunlight, or long, dark hair that flowed down
to their narrow waists, or short, boyish cuts that caught in
damp curls against their foreheads. Most of the men had
mustaches or beards; they looked like brothers from an enormous family. Paul was in the midst of them, shouting, and
Helen's heart sank. This had happened before, in April,
when the bikers brought a petition asking support for a bike
trail along the old Illinois Central right-of-way. Paul refused
to sign, and long after the railroad had given the land to the
county he was still furious—had tried to form a committee
with other farmers, but gave up when Jess Eriksen accused
him of wanting to lead "a goddamn bunch of vigilantes."
Only Harvey Riker had been on Paul's side.

She parked the pickup in the shade of the barn and approached the group.

"I've got a living to make," she heard Paul say. "You think it makes me happy to see good farmland wasted?"

"It's already done," one of the bikers said. "The county's already made it a bike trail. All we're asking is for you to meet us halfway—respect our right to use it and help us protect it."

Now Helen could see they were not all young people. They were of various ages—late teens to late thirties—and they were serious-faced, intent.

"A strip of land that size might make the difference between profit and loss for me someday," Paul said. "Next spring I've got to plant fence line to fence line. If this year doesn't put me in the poorhouse."

A bearded man nearby turned his front wheel toward Helen and winked. "Farmers," he said. "I've never met one yet that wasn't losing his shirt. They only keep farming because it's so much fun."

She wondered whether or not to be angry with him. "I'm his wife," she said. "You have to understand that he's telling the truth. That land was his—at least, it was his grandfather's —before the railroad needed it."

"This is only about the bridge," the bearded man said, "the I.C. bridge over the West Fork. Some farmers out in Winthrop set fire to a bridge just like it, really wasted it. We're talking to all the farmers around here, asking them to keep an eye out for that kind of thing."

"My husband's not one of your fans," Helen said.

"We're not asking him to love us. Just live and let live."

Helen smiled at him, liking him. "That seems simple enough."

She went on to the house, put the mail on the table and the six-pack into the refrigerator. The air in the kitchen was humid with canning heat. A solitary fly buzzed against one of the windows. "Wasted," the young man had said, and she wondered if he had been in Vietnam, one of the lucky ones who came back unhurt. She went upstairs and changed into

a pair of blue shorts she would never have considered wearing
outside the house and came back down to the kitchen. Paul
was standing at the door, looking out. The bicyclists were just
turning onto the gravel road, bent over their handlebars like
jockeys, a glitter of sun dancing off their machines.

"What do you think of that?" Paul said.

"I think it was polite of them to talk to you."

"You know what's going to happen," he said. "Kids litter-
ing the place with trash from McDonald's, soda cans, candy
wrappers. Wrecking the fences."

"They aren't all kids," she said. "Some of them are nearly
as old as you or me."

"Second childhood," Paul said. "Then we'll have beer cans
along with the soda cans, and condoms instead of candy wrappers."

He went to the refrigerator, took out one of the cans of
beer she had just put in.

"That'll be warm," she said.

He opened it anyway. "What's a strip of dirt mean to somebody who can spend three, four hundred dollars on one of
those fancy bicycles?" he said.

"Oh, Paul . . . " But words to argue with him wouldn't
come—as if she couldn't betray him even when she wished
to.

"I know," he said. He sat heavily and laid his cap on the
table. "It isn't like me to bitch all the time."

"It's the drought," she said.

"It's everything. I chopped that field this morning and just
got madder and madder. I thought, Five or six weeks from
now we'll get a damned foot of rain, and it'll be too late. Just
like this spring: so much rain I couldn't go into the fields to
put the seed in."

He took a drink from the warm can and made a face.

"What I know is, I need land one whole hell of a lot more
than a bunch of overgrown babies on two-wheelers."

"You'll have the PIK money," she said.

"And that's a joke." He gave her a look that was nearly scornful. "I didn't have the brains to set aside that much, and anyway, it's the big company farms that'll rake in most of the PIK money, and the grain dealers that'll get rich, handling corn from five years ago all over again."

He set the beer can aside.

"It's the principle of the thing," he said. "President Franklin Pierce gave this land to my great-great-grandfather—the only decent thing the government ever did for the Tobler family. No one ought to ask me to give it up—not any of it."

"It's such a tiny bit."

"I don't care if it's no bigger than a postage stamp." He put on the cap and yanked its bill down over his eyes. "I'm going into town, where the beer's cold," he said.

But the bike trail doesn't matter, she wanted to say, watching him climb into the cab of the pickup, hearing him grind the gears in frustration. It's the weather and the government both, and you can't beat either one of them.

For the rest of the day she tried to keep busy with odd jobs. She hauled the sealed Mason jars down to the basement and shelved them alongside the green beans she had done the summer before. She thought about the young man who was probably a Vietnam veteran, and how fortunate it was that Peter had been too young for that war. She did the laundry, though she might have put it off another day or two, and got out the mending basket to do some odds and ends she had been saving for cooler weather. Once she looked up from sewing a shirt button to see that the light had changed sharply. Clouds, she imagined. In the excitement of thinking there might be rain, she went outside for a moment to look westward; but it was simply dust in the air.

It was not like Paul to solve his problems by drowning them. To have a few drinks, that was all right, but he hated to be drunk, to feel he had given up control. What he liked —and it mostly amused her—was to clown with her, to giggle, make bad jokes, pat her buttocks. But lately . . . She could not say what had changed. Something that frightened her, a desperation, a willfulness. Dear heaven, if I can't put my mind on something pleasant, I'll start inventing trouble when there's already plenty to go around.

One summer, when the children were still young and at home, still interested enough in horses to feed and groom them as well as ride them, Helen took them to Kentucky, to the marvelous green expanse of the world around Lexington, to visit the horse farms. Paul had not gone—couldn't go, he said; the land needed him.

The second day she drove to Calumet Farm, still full of the pleasure of Walnut Hall the day before, where Sarah and Peter had driven a foreman crazy with questions. Walnut Hall didn't breed racehorses; the children—Peter especially—had begged for Calumet, but when the three of them arrived at the Calumet gate they were stopped by a sign: NO VISITORS. Sarah took the matter calmly, acidly: "If they think they're too good for us, that's fine with me." Peter whined. Helen was disappointed. Beyond the forbidden entrance they could see white buildings trimmed in red, with red-roofed cupolas. "So near and yet so far," she said to Sarah.

In Lexington she tried to make up for the morning's failure by taking the children to a fancy restaurant, but there was no forgetting. Peter was impossible, Sarah merely petulant. After the dismal lunch she went to a public telephone and looked up the Calumet number in the book.

"I'm terribly sorry," said the woman who answered the phone. "Calumet Farm is open for persons in the horse business—not for tourists."

"I'm here with my two children," Helen said. "We drove all the way from Iowa. As it happens, we own a quarter horse named Cloud and a part-Thoroughbred named Lopez. Does that put us in the horse business?"

There had been a lovely silence.

"You-all come on ahead," the woman said. "Park at the main office and I'll find a man to show you around."

Then they had been everywhere except the breeding barns —the stables, the tack rooms, the meadows surrounding. In Helen's memory the fences were an astonishing white, the trim of the buildings a dark, perfect red, the bluegrass deep and green. She and the children had reached through the rails to stroke the blazes of chestnut-colored yearlings with names engraved on brass plates riveted to their halter straps: Sunglint, Morning Sun—names she had never forgotten. And even grown up and scattered, Sarah and Peter remembered Citation, a Triple Crown winner—an enormous bay stallion, nearly twenty-five, shambling alongside his groom like a solemn old man lost in his memories. Years after, when she read of Citation's death, Helen had wanted to cry, had left the room so Paul wouldn't question her.

That wonderful summer. Traveling without Paul, coping with the two children, gaining them entry to a forbidden place. It had been the proudest and happiest event of all her married life.

She woke up in the black of night, alone in the bed. Paul's side had not been slept in; neither his warmth nor his reassuring man's smell was on the bedclothes. She imagined him sitting in the D-Town Tap, drinking beer and quarreling with the others—farmers, some of them, but laid-off factory workers too, and truckers between hauls—a small army of men whose occupations had lost their value or vanished entirely. Sensible family men getting drunk.

She looked at the alarm clock, on the nightstand on Paul's side of the bed. Its greenish-yellow hands showed nearly four o'clock. The Tap closed at two. If he'd gone off to play pepper with his usual cronies, he would never have stayed out so late. He wasn't the sort to sit in a pickup on a back road and drink beer with a buddy—hadn't done such a thing since coming home from Korea, thirty years ago.

She got out of bed and went to the bathroom. In the harsh glare of the overhead light she closed her eyes and touched the lids with her fingers. Her hands were hot on her cheeks; the nightgown clung to her back and sides. It used to be that you could depend on the nights to cool down. It used to be that you closed the doors so you and your husband could say silly words to each other in whispers that wouldn't alert the children—to what? To the secret that you cared more for each other than for weather and work?

She tidied herself, turned out the light, went through the hallway and gingerly down the front staircase. This year everything was weather. The sun, dry days, a crying need for rain. The dust would be far worse when the farmers in Kansas and Nebraska did their fall plowing. Then in late September and October she would notice the whole western sky dark orange—like the eerie approach of a tornado—and for days the tawny dust would be thick on everything: cars and trucks and machinery, windowsills and porch railings. When it rained—and finally it would pour, Paul was right—if you caught the rain in a bucket or pan, it would be murky with Plains dirt. All those concerns lay between Paul and herself. Those and more: practical matters like credit at the Farm Fleet, credit for parts needed to overhaul the machinery in time for spring plowing and planting. And what to plant, how much to plant, what would the government do next? Helen understood without being able to tell Paul—in Paul's language—that what absorbed and frightened him likewise frightened her.

Dear Paul.

She felt her way down the front hall, unlatched the screen door and stepped onto the porch. A slight, warm breeze brushed across her face and bare arms, and sighed in the branches of the nearest ash. Too early for the robins. The night was almost black; there was no moon—but off to the

east she saw the glow of light that was Waterloo, and south
of that the lesser glow that must be Vinton, and due south
from where she stood a throbbing of light she could not at
first make sense of. It seemed to be—it was—where the old
I.C. right-of-way met the West Fork. *Dear Paul.* She wanted
the light to be . . . anything safe. A campfire, a bonfire
tended by some of the college students having a kegger to
celebrate the beginning of classes. False dawn.

She went back to bed to wait. Certainly she knew the old
railroad bridge was burning, and her husband was too simple
and direct not to have done it—probably with Harvey, the
two of them drunk and angry after the Tap closed up. And
how easy it would have been, how thorough. She had seen
fence posts, kindled by spring fires set in the roadside ditches,
that burned for days, slowly and to the heart, and she imagined the timbers of the bridge—black with creosote, dry with
age—smoldering long after the fire-department volunteers
had done all they knew to do. She could imagine the seeds of
flame growing in the scars carved by axes and chisels when
the bridge was built, and the charred wood steaming when
the first rains touched it. O the things we say we love, she
told herself—dozing and waking in the stifling room—and
the things we do to prove it.

She got up for good at six-thirty and made coffee from the
Colombian beans, standing at the sink to watch the misty
light dissipate in the fields. Paul was not home; there was no
telling when he would appear, whether he would be sheepish
or arrogant, whether he might have Harvey Riker with him
—to soften the consequences of what he had done, the way a
boy brings home a friend to shame his mother out of her
anger. Yet she might be mistaken, jumping to wrong conclu-
sions. And even if she was right, the worst of that was the
way Paul would expect her to take his side, see his reasons,
help him explain. He would never see that he was trying to
lead her to a place where she ought not to follow. What
should she do, she wondered, for this unhappy man?

When the sheriff's car came down the gravel road from the east, kicking up the dust that would add one more layer of white to the weed leaves and stems, Helen thought at first it was the Jehovah's Witness lady in the gold Cadillac. *As if I'd tell her what I really believe.* Then she saw the bubble of light on the roof and recognized the county shield on the front door. She watched the car stop near the toolshed; watched the young deputy stride toward her in his morning-fresh khakis. *As if I'd tell anybody.*

Nam

One Monday morning he has parked the car across the street from a schoolyard and sits, smoking cigarettes and watching the children. I see him from two cross-streets away, a shadow in the window on the passenger side; the car is idling, has never been shut off, the exhaust on this day in October a thin blueness in sunlight. Now it is recess time, the schoolyard filled with children running, swinging, playing with a football. I tap on the closed window beside his head. Three, four times, and finally he turns his face toward me.

I think how I haven't gotten used to his eyes; not yet. They are not vacant, not wild, but something of each, as if he sees something both dimensioned and dimensionless, something that angers him without provoking him. Today, recognizing me, he winks.

"Roll down the window," I say, making the circular motion with my right hand. He cocks his head, the cigarette at the corner of his mouth. I point downward, meaning to direct his attention to the window crank. I form Roll down the window with my mouth, but don't utter the words.

He shakes his head. He looks through me, watching the children beyond the low chain-link fence of the schoolyard.

I walk to the other side of the car, fumble in my purse for the keys, unlock the driver's-side door, and slide onto the front seat beside him.

"Hi," I say.

"Fancy meeting you here," he says. He opens the window to throw away the consumed cigarette, closes it, lights another Lucky Strike.

"They called me from work. They said you left just after you punched in."

"True." He nods, shrugs. "You know."

"I wanted to be sure you were okay."

"Why shouldn't I be?" He turns his mad-blank gaze toward me. "Why shouldn't I be okay?"

I feel my fingers tighten on the lower rim of the steering wheel. Is this the day? The voice—not my own, but stronger, portentous, perhaps my father's, my mother's, my doctor's—hisses inside my head. Is this the day?

He talks about the children.

"You see that one," he says, "the little girl in the camel coat, the girl with the red mittens: when she grows up she's going to be a ringer for Elizabeth Taylor, a dead ringer." He looks at me. "You see her?"

"Yes."

"You know—you just know—that if you could get close to her and turn her face so you could look, you just know she'd have green eyes."

"Yes."

He slumps a little in the seat beside me. "Irish," he says.

"A colleen," I say.

He turns his head quickly, staring at me, past me, out the window into the mid-morning sun that probably silhouettes me, makes me difficult to read. If he were a stranger, I would think I had offended him.

"A dead ringer," he says.

We have no children of our own. It is an agreement—a contract—we arrived at long ago, ten years ago, the day I met him at the bus station and clung to him and wept tears I had saved nearly all the months he was gone.

"I will never enter you," he said, whispering in my ear. "Never. I will do anything else, anything you want, but never that."

He is compulsive about his promises. At night, in the dark, we are animal and violent, erotic and despairing. No part of my body but knows his mouth, his hands, the extraordinary heat of him.

Times when he has gone for days without shaving, his beard abrades me; I stand before the mirror on the bathroom door and rub lotion into the rawness of my breasts, my stomach, my thighs. Sometimes he uses his teeth; one night I pushed him away and ran into the lighted hallway, appalled to see the glistening of my own blood. He worships me. He devours me. He will not have me bring children into this horrid world.

He knows that when he went away to war I was pregnant, and he knows I miscarried the child in a dream—a nightmare —on the very night of his killing the first of the enemy he encountered. It frightens him, this connection. He has told me he finds something in it that is occult, impossible. He tells me that when things are bad, really bad, he imagines even now our baby perished because the man he cut in half with his automatic weapon was thinking of it—was thinking, How can this American murder me even while he is dreaming of a son? He tells me perhaps this is what interferes with his "rehabilitation"—this perilous angry struggle between creator and killer.

I hold him then. Some nights I sing to him, soft melodies I might have sung to the baby if it had survived the delicate anatomies I am made of. When he is calm, when I am no longer chilled where his mouth has grazed, then I return the pleasure, the wildness, in my own manner. I see him smile in the half-light from the hall. He calls me Mother Thumb.

My mother argues that I should save my tears. "The man isn't worth the expense of them" is the way she puts it. My father, when he is there to listen to us, makes jokes about "save" and "expense" and tells us he is ashamed of us for our mercenary way of talking. My father was a sergeant in the Second War; he understands perfectly what my husband is suffering—shell shock. He has known a half-dozen men like my husband; nothing can be done. "Just keep an eye on him." Time diminishes the problem, he tells me. "But don't let him have a gun," he says. "You don't keep a gun, do you?" I tell my father No, we have never kept a gun. I resent my father at times like this; whatever he may be, my husband is no madman, no lunatic who will—as they say—"go berserk" in some populated place.

Now, sitting in silence outside the fence around the school, the engine idling, the voices of the children blocked by the closed windows and smothered by the engine noise, I am not so sure Elizabeth Taylor has green eyes.

"Didn't we see them in a magazine once? Weren't they violet?"

He lights a cigarette. "Violet," he echoes.

"Don't you remember? A close-up—the pupils were very small, and the color around them was like crushed glass, purplish and splintery."

"Vaguely," he says. "I vaguely remember."

Close-up: it is a word that makes him pensive. He tells me that when he dreams, all the violence of his Asian war has been drained away, and what remain are slow images: faces, houses, natural objects. He says it is as if someone unseen is laying out a succession of photographs on a long table, and each photograph is extraordinary in its detail. Everything is seen in close-up. Everything seems larger than life. He told me once—quite recently—that he thought all the pictures he has dreamed for ten years could be put together like a vast jigsaw puzzle, and that the puzzle would be a total panorama of his time in the jungles and rank villages, an incredible scrapbook of all the people, living and dead, he saw there.

It is this suspended quality of his life—this stasis—that more and more perplexes me as time passes. Ten years ago we shared hours of activity: talking, traveling about, lovemaking in our curious fashions. Now we communicate less, move about less, love angrily. We are each drifting, but in opposite directions. If I look at him, I see him shrinking, smaller and smaller, into himself. I think before very long he will be so distant as to be faceless; I think someday I will not even recognize him as the man I married.

Then I think perhaps we are not growing more distant from each other, but only wasting away to nothing because time is swallowing us. We sustain ourselves out of whatever storehouses of self-sufficiency we have; eventually we will vanish forever.

We sit. The children empty the schoolyard. What I need to do is persuade him out of himself, coax him to talk—like lancing an infection, my doctor advises me, letting out the poisons. Do the poisons then dissipate? Or are they like the color-named herbicide that devastated the jungles we are haunted by—seeming to fade, but turning secret and lethal in the blood and bones of men and the children they thought-lessly father?

I say: "Do you want to quit?"

"Quit what? The job?" He grins, studies his cigarette. "And do nothing all day?"

"Or take another job."

"I'd rather do nothing."

Probably. I have watched him work—was allowed one morning to stand at the glass wall of an office and see him packing the round lids for five-gallon ice cream containers. Behind him two women sat at machines that crimped alumi-num rims onto the lids; great silver skeins of metal hung like wreaths beyond them, and the finished lids dropped into the waiting boxes—two, four, six, eight—eternally. "He can't keep up," I said. The plant manager smiled at me. "They're on piecework, those ladies," he said.

When the two women stopped for the mid-morning break, he went on packing—sealing the full cartons, stacking them on skids, ready for a forklift to carry them five high to the loading dock. By the time the women finished their cigarettes and came back to the machines, he was caught up. He would catch up again at lunch, again at the afternoon break, again in fifteen or twenty minutes past the end of his shift.

"I don't have time to think," he told me once. "That's the glory of the place."

He cuts his hands over and over again on the shiny metal of the rims and the edges of sealing tape. He laughs, telling me about the smears of blood he leaves on the cardboard lids. "Raspberry flavor only," he says.

I stay with him. In spite of everything—his distance, his silence, his cruelty to himself—I stay. Not to understand, surely. Not to help. And if it comes to that, who helps me?

The engine idles. Soon the gas tank will be empty, the car will stall. We will sit here listening to the sounds metal makes cooling down; it will be like music. Our breath will cloud the windows, and the odor of tobacco will be suffocating. Eventually he will get out of the car and walk away. A man in coveralls will appear from somewhere, carrying a red can of gasoline. I will drive home alone.

"What are you thinking?" I say.

He shakes his head.

Now the children reappear—lunchtime. Most of them leave the schoolyard, come past the car shouting and laughing, chasing. They pay no attention to us. A dozen or so of their playmates remain on the schoolyard; a knot of boys gathers near the swings.

"Did I tell you about my prisoner?"

"No," I say. The truth. He has told me about killing. He has told me time and again about terror. He has told me how many fires he set to destroy how many villages.

"He'd lived in China; I'm not even sure he wasn't Chinese —some kind of advisor, a liaison. He spoke perfect English."

"How did you capture him?"

"He gave himself up to me—it wasn't anything I did. He came out of the hut alone. His hands weren't over his head; they were held away from his sides, as if he was going to embrace me. He wanted to show me he wasn't hiding anything. He was wearing a khaki uniform—that was unusual— and a belt with a leather holster at his waist. The pistol was in his right hand; he held it out to me, the grip toward me. 'Take it,' he said. 'Use it.' "

"What did you do?"

"I took it. I released the clip and emptied the chamber onto the ground. I threw the pistol off into the brush." He lays his forehead against the window beside him. "I hope he survived all the interrogations."

"Probably he did."

"He was full of stories. About China—about old wars and about flooding and about famines and plagues. He taught history, he said. Every story he told me was like a fairy tale. Not that you couldn't believe it, but that if you believed it you had to believe it was more than a story. Did I tell about the babies?"

"No," I say. " I haven't heard any of this."

"There was a famine. People were dying of hunger, so when babies were born there was nothing to feed them with. The mothers were starving; they couldn't make milk. What they did was take each new baby to a ruined palace that overlooked the village from a high cliff and lay it on a windowsill. The walls were two or three feet thick, which meant there was room for several babies. Every time a new mother put her baby on the sill, it pushed the furthest child off the edge. No mother ever killed her own baby, and no mother ever knew whose baby she killed."

He looks at me.

"Neat," I say.

His eyes are blank.

A commotion near the schoolyard swings draws us away from our thoughts, our visions. It is a fight; two boys are squared off, their small fists clenched, their faces angry. The others— they are all boys but one—are a rough circle around them. Punches are thrown; the bystanders encourage the fighting. We can hear the shouts even above the drumming of the engine.

"What do they think they're doing?" my husband says. He flings the car door angrily open; rather than run to the school-yard entrance, he goes straight to the chain-link fence and vaults it. He confronts the children. I draw the car door closed to keep out the cold and watch from my safe distance.

He has stepped between the two adversaries, one hand on the shoulder of the smaller, the other against the chest of the taller. He talks to them by turns. Once or twice he seems to be addressing the onlookers. I see on all their faces petulance, disgust. Some of them wander away from the swings, hands in pockets, feet kicking at schoolyard rocks.

Now he persuades the two fighters to shake hands; the gesture may be grudging, but it suffices. For the first time I notice blood on the face of one of the boys.

The group disperses. Only the girl remains, and of course it is the girl in the camel coat who will grow up to look like Elizabeth Taylor. She speaks to him; he nods. He puts out his hands to her, rests them on her narrow shoulders, says something and laughs. A man—a teacher?—appears in the schoolhouse doorway. He and my husband exchange words, wave, separate.

"A little nosebleed," he tells me.

"Something to do with the green-eyed girl?"

"Something," he says. "Or nothing."

"Are her eyes really green?"

He slumps in the seat. "I couldn't tell," he says, and all in a moment he is crying, his hands over his face, his body turned against the door.

I know better than to touch him. I understand not to say anything to comfort him. Instead I gaze out the misted window, my mind filled with the colors of blood and glass, the images of men and children dying from great height, the haplessness of women too hollow to make milk or keep their babies. Is this the day? the familiar voice sighs. Is every day the day?

Praises

Not long after the extraordinary success of the Grand Exhibition, he flew to Europe by himself and moved into a small apartment in Copenhagen: three rooms in a narrow street off the Gothersgade. Looking for a place, he had held in mind the incandescent memory of the year after the war, when he had lived in Paris in a room with casement windows. Waking at sunrise, he could look across to the towers of the Notre-Dame, and—if the night before he had set the right-hand window at the correct angle—admire the wavering reflection of the Sainte-Chapelle in the opened-out glass portal. Unpacking books and the single Giacometti statuette his New York agent had given him to commemorate the Exhibition, he remembered one Paris winter morning—cobwebs of new snow caught in the window corners and between the stones of Notre-Dame; the Sainte-Chapelle half-hidden under wings of frost. The chill of the bare floor made him seem to fly to the window, and his breath was palpable. He was at the casement, leaning out to draw the windows shut, when a bright orange cat appeared on the sill and leaped past him into the room. He could see its small tracks in the snow of the roof, and when he returned to bed the cat was already nestled against the breasts of the young woman he was living with at the time. Its paw prints had marked the yellowing sheets like a trail of flowers.

Now that he was located, some of his books shelved and the Giacometti placed on a mantelpiece where it was made to appear less solitary by the mirror behind it, he stood tying his necktie, his lips pursed like a man about to begin whistling. The expression on his face so struck him that he became self-conscious and could not make the knot come out properly. He untangled the ends of the necktie and began over, but the more he concentrated on the act of tying— over, around, under, through—the more difficult the matter became.

It might have been forty years earlier, at an army base in Texas, when he was the only man in his barracks who understood the art of the necktie. To his infantry comrades—all of them Texans—it was a talent that seemed bizarre. In the end it was his ticket into their friendship and acceptance. On a Sunday during basic training, the platoon's first trip into El Paso, he was surrounded by eager men with sunburnt throats exposed, and for an hour he stood, creating perfect knots and reciting aloud the hand movements he required them to commit to memory. He remembered their lips moving soundlessly —*over, around, under, through*—to learn that new skill. When all of them had returned by midnight, drunk or dazed and once more open-collared, they woke him and proclaimed him an honorary Texan, swearing to take him to Mexico when the army issued their first three-day passes.

But it was merely a matter of not thinking about the act. If you thought—if you said to yourself: What am I doing? and What am I doing now?—then the thing couldn't be done.

The army, the war, taught him kinesthesia, and the lesson kept him alive; but after the army it had taken him years to learn to keep faith with the lesson: the muscles think for themselves, and you do not throw your paints aside in frustration, or dwell upon the changes in your face.

This time of day in September, the northern sun rode near the horizon. He imagined its rays slanting in upon the supper tables of the Danes, burnishing the tableware, turning every room a gold whose diminishing would come so gradually that none would notice until someone seated furthest from the windows asked to have a lamp turned on. He had always thought such late light contradictory—not sufficient for the finework his present reputation rested on, but more than enough for the great polygons of color which had finally brought him to the attention of important men and women. He had always wanted fame, daydreamed it, and when, later, he began to realize it, he was astonished and relieved. Only when he was alone and tired might he admit that he was a lesser figure than Picasso dancing a jig or Stravinsky playing solitaire or Max Ernst confessing he could not recall in which language he had most recently dreamed.

At the entrance to the Magasin du Nord a couple caught his interest: a man gray, distinguished, his own age; a woman youthful, chestnut-haired. That might have been himself with any of the young women he had in his lifetime loved but hardly known—like that diligent child the week before the Exhibition, the one he had watched searching his canvases for flaws, recording in a spiral notebook each scratch, each pinhole, each blemish of time or carelessness against the claims of the paintings' owners. "How scrupulous you are!" he had said to her. And later, lying with her, he had wondered that her attentiveness to the artist was less scrupulous than her concern for his works. Was it envy he felt for other men's women?

Before his army unit left camp, basic training finished and the battlefields of North Europe ahead of them, there had been a celebration: Early Times and Lone Star and rowdy Texas music. He had sat in the second-floor bay of the barracks, nursing a water glass filled with bourbon. One of his comrades played steel guitar. The men whooped and sang, drank and punched at one another; a poker game went on in the sergeant's quarters at the far end of the bay; heat lay on everything, drawing sweat out of the men, the tumblers of liquor, the beer cans. Soldiers stripped off their khaki shirts, their undershirts; sat in opened windows or leaned idly against their bunks. They wiped their hands, cool from the drinks they held, across their chests and stomachs.

Someone brought in a woman. She was a whore—she could not have been anything else—but she was young, attractive. No one knew how she was smuggled into camp, past the guards at the gate. No one knew whose woman she was, so she was everyone's: all of them danced with her, gave her whiskey to drink, kissed her, helped to undress her like a child's doll. By then she was helpless, giddy, laughing at everything. "She won't remember," the sergeant said carelessly.

He watched. He had even been excited by the watching, and in the small hours of the morning he climbed to his upper bunk and fell asleep, drunk and frustrated, with the music of the steel and the woman's broken laughter for lullaby.

In the light of day he was the first man up. The barracks was golden with dust and low sunlight, a litter of cans, papers, a torn deck of cards, an empty bottle balanced on a fire extinguisher. The woman was still there, asleep, and he dressed and went to her. She was slumped against the wall under an open window, mouth slack, her legs carelessly splayed. No one had troubled to cover her; her dark skin was beaded with sweat, her black hair matted and damp; she looked not real, like a broken mannequin. The floor under her thighs was wet. A cigarette butt was soggy in the puddle.

Reefer. He looked around for her clothes. They were every-where, it seemed. He gathered up as many as he could find and knelt beside her, touched her shoulder. She shivered and opened her eyes—brown eyes, the whites bloodshot.

For a moment she had looked at him as if she expected to be able to call him by name. "What time is it?" she said.

"After six."

"Do you have my money?"

"I don't know about any money."

She looked down at herself, down at the wet floor. "Who did that?" she said. "Did I?"

"I picked up your clothes. Most of them."

She took them. Then she hid her face in the bundle of clothing and wept.

He had not known what to do to stop her crying, except to reach out and hold her like a child, and rock her in his arms until she was quiet.

In front of the Royal Theater, its baroque façade, its array of statues, he paused to read the bill. Tomorrow, he saw, a famous pianist was to appear, and tonight was a stage play whose name, in Danish, he did not recognize. He was about to turn away, to walk back toward the Raadhusplads perhaps for a whiskey at a quiet café, when the second item on the evening's program halted him: a ballet whose music, by Milhaud, he knew well. He had never seen the piece danced.

The lobby of the theater was not crowded; at the box office, a short line—a portly gentleman, several schoolchildren—bought tickets and moved away.

"A ticket," he told the cashier. He held up a forefinger. "For this evening."

The cashier, a woman, fiftyish, peered at him and leaned forward.

"Are you English?"

"American."

"Do you speak Dansk?"

He shook his head. "I don't know Danish."

"Then why do you wish a ticket?"

"To see the ballet—the Milhaud."

She considered him. "I think it would be a mistake. First is a play in Danish. A very long play. If you speak no Danish, you will be uncomfortable; nothing will be comprehensible."

"Please," he said. "One ticket."

"I think not. You would think badly of me, and have boring memories of Copenhagen."

"If I promise not to take my seat until the play is over . . . ?"

"Please," she said. "You will thank me."

He turned away from the cage. Partly he was amused, partly annoyed. In New York he would have remarked to his agent that he hoped to attend a show, a concert, an exhibit, and with one phone call she would have arranged for tickets. No cross-examination about the competence of the purchaser to understand the performance, for who in such a world would ever be allowed into an art gallery? I should say to her: *What is the language of dance?* and he stood, irresolute, wondering if it mattered so much that he see the ballet performed.

His indecision was interrupted by the sound of his own name—as plain as that: his name. Only later did he recall how it was freighted with resonances of time past. A woman's voice. Coming amid the wry amusement of his failure to buy a theater ticket, the voice seemed to connect itself to his unspoken question: What is the language of dance? as if it were itself the answer. My name. The woman's voice repeated it.

"It is you, isn't it?" she said.

"Yes," he said. "My God, yes."

"I've been watching you out of the shadows. I said to myself: I know that distinguished-looking man. Then the question was: Will he know me?" She tipped her head, looked hard at him; her eyes were pale gray. "You know how silly one feels accosting a person who turns out to be a stranger."

"I don't know what to say."

"You might say you're glad to see me, never mind the passage of the years—that sort of thing." She paused. "Unless you're not," she said.

"I am." He took her hands—small, cool—in his. "I'm stunned," he said. "Do you have any time? Can we go somewhere and talk?"

She took his arm, leaned against him to steer him out of the theater.

"One glass of wine," she said, "then I have to be at the hotel for dinner." She raised her free hand to silence him. "I know. We surely can't cover twenty years over a drink."

"Tomorrow," he said.

"Tomorrow evening I'm back in Sussex. But come along; I know a place. My host introduced me to it yesterday." She steered him across the Bredgade. It was a gesture as casual as if they had seen each other only the day before.

"How long have you been here?"

"Days and days," she said. "Four, to be precise."

The notion that he and she might have been spending these four days together—after years when he had hardly thought of her—disturbed him. "Where are you staying?"

"The Palace. You?"

"No—I was there for a while. I've just rented a place not far from here."

"Rented? You're living in Copenhagen?"

"I thought for a while. A little vacation." He glanced sidelong at her. "Were you going to the theater?"

"No. Deciding not to. Turning back a ticket for tomorrow's concert." She pointed to a restaurant canopy not far ahead. "That's where we're going."

"Can you have dinner?"

"I told you: I'm engaged for dinner."

He held the door for her; inside—a dim lobby—he stood beside her as the host approached. He felt, though he could not have said why, a sense of having found, for the first time in a long time, a proper companion.

"I think I've been in this place," he said. "A long time back."

"Yes," she said. "Life is all coincidences, isn't it?" And by then she was preceding him to a table near a window.

Of course she had changed. It was not only that she was older, but as if the years—and distance, and her success, which more than matched his own—had taken her out of context, so that he did not know her in these clothes, in this setting. Her mouth was thinner, her face pale, the cheekbones more prominent; the straight line of the lips suggested less patience with the world.

"Of all places," she said.

"I visited here after the war. I used to tell you about it—how it seemed like an oasis of English in a desert of European."

"Does it still?"

He told her his adventure at the theater box office. She laughed with him, not once taking her eyes from his face.

"And what about you?" he said.

"One of my books is going into a Danish edition. I came over to let myself be made much of." She put it wryly, as if however much she wished to take seriously the being-made-of, she could not quite carry it off.

"Has it been pleasant?"

She looked away from him, the light through the café windows illuminating the right side of her face. He saw how clear-skinned she was now—she had fretted in her youth among doctors and hormone injections and delicately hurtful surgeries—and how her dark hair was shot through with gray. Forty-something, she would be.

"I'm of two minds," she said. "I'm flattered by the attentions I'm given. I'm impatient to get back time for myself."

He nodded.

"I never get used to it—though I imagine it's worse for you than for me. You were always rather less gregarious."

"How do you know I haven't reformed?" he said.

She smiled. The smile made her more familiar, the remembered girl emerging out of the somewhat formal woman. "Not likely," she said. "I've kept up with you, more or less. When I'm in New York, I drop into that little gallery of yours—the one up on Seventy-seventh?—to see what you've been doing."

"Not much lately."

"Some artistic doldrum?" She sipped at the wine. "This is a lovely claret," she said. And then: "I'd have thought the huge success of your retrospective might have renewed you. Revved you up."

"I've kept track of you, too," he said. "Though maybe not as closely as I should have."

"In what way have you?"

"The truth is," he said, "once I went to a movie that was adapted from a book of yours. It must have been nine or ten years ago. I went because somebody said it was about you and me."

"And was it?"

He looked down at her hands, which idly turned the stem of the wineglass. "I wasn't sure. Afterward—thinking about it—I supposed it was."

"We write what we know," she said. "Or what we should have known if only we'd thought of it in time."

He lifted his gaze to her face.

"The French call it *l'esprit d'escalier*," she said. "Why are you looking at me in that odd way? Trying to catch out the old me in spite of twenty years?"

"You're quite lovely; amazingly young-looking."

"My word." She shook her head in apparent wonder. "You're distressingly the same man. What next? An accidental brushing of my hand? A flustered apology?"

"Really . . ."

"Besides, it's only the magic of modern chemistry," she said. And then she hesitated; her tone of voice softened. "I'm sorry. There—I'm the one apologizing. I don't have any special reason to be defensive with you, do I?"

"I hope not."

"I do intend not to let us be carried away by nostalgia. Yes, I think I've held up nicely against ravaging time. But it truly is chemical. When I decided to go on the pill—I don't recall if that convenience was available to us in the olden days— my complexion miraculously cleared. By the time I was frightened out of taking it, I'd outgrown bad skin. Or so it seems."

"You never married." He did not make it a question.

"Never," she said. "I learned from your bad example."

He looked out the window into the twilight. The street was busy. Playgoers, he imagined, all fluent in the necessary language.

"And you never remarried," she said. "You never found Mother."

He laughed.

"You didn't always think it was so funny. It made you rather curiously—respectful. In bed. I've not met anyone since who was quite so pious about love."

"And I haven't met anyone so impiously honest."

"When we choose to live alone, we become ever so much more what we innately are."

"You sound very English."

"That too. What I innately am."

"I used to wonder why you decided to live outside the country."

"I don't live 'outside' the country," she said. "England is one, after all. But I'm still a U.S. citizen; I go back every couple of years, and feel . . . I don't know. I suppose I feel a little bit foreign, a little bit the outsider in spite of my official loyalty. One gains a perspective. You know; you've lived abroad."

"But I never went native," he said.

She measured him with her look. "You're as flippant with me as ever, aren't you?" she said. "Something was always wrong with the way you dealt with me when we lived together. It must still have to do with the difference in our ages —your consciousness of it, your embarrassment over it. The years do put you off your balance." She pushed her glass toward him for refilling. "Though as I come to think of it, your tragic pose—your romanticism—was what most attracted me. It excited my girlish sympathies."

He waited.

"I appear to have given considerable thought to you," she said. "More than you gave to me, I should guess." She set the glass aside. "Suffice it that you never understood how serious I was. Even in three years you never appreciated how I used to respond to you, to that way you had of taking me over— bundling me into the dark of your carnal imagination. Or how I hoped and prayed you didn't think me easy. 'O God,' I used to say in bed at night, 'please don't let me lose him because he wasn't the first to have me.' " She took a cigarette out of her purse but made no move to light it. "You didn't know I was that silly, did you?"

"Not ever." He closed his eyes; saw a young woman across the bed in her studio apartment, saw his hands unbuttoning her, her arms outspread like a child angel's in the snow of the bedclothes. *Respectful,* she called him. The first time he loved her, how deep her climax went, down to the marrow of all her bones. Such happiness he felt.

"I remember our first time," he said.

She lighted the cigarette. "I was always trying so damned hard to please you," she said. "You have to take into account the differences between us. My only experience was with men —boys, really—of my own generation. Callow, clumsy. And here you were: twice my age, on your way to success, not some fool of a child only wanting to wet a finger in me. You've no idea how reassuring you were."

"Really I was terrified. Of moving in with you. Of . . . "
He paused. "A number of things."

"Certainly I know that now—found it out before your Dr.
Whatsis did—but at the first, you seemed like a Gibraltar.
'What on earth does he see in me?' I used to ask myself. I
counted myself incredibly fortunate." She stubbed out the
scarcely smoked cigarette.

"But then there was the scales-from-my-eyes phase. Here I
was, sleeping with a married man, and what was finally going
to happen? Would he divorce the wicked witch and marry
the princess? Would he ditch her when he was tired of her?
Would she get pregnant and perish under the knife of some
back-street abortionist? Or, worse, would she have the child,
which would of course be a boy, and go through life haunted
by the image of her undoing? You see? First I thought
about you—noble me. Then I thought about me—ignoble
you."

"You make it sound miserable," he said.

"I used to lie beside you after you'd gone to sleep," she said,
"and I'd hold your left hand against my mouth, kiss your
fingers—and taste your wedding ring. Do you know what it
tasted like? It tasted like the iron railing at the entrance of
the school where I went to kindergarten. Anyway, I'd taste
the ring, and I'd cry as softly as soft can be . . . And now,
looking back, a huge part of my memory of you is the taste of
metal and salt.

"I don't know what I thought. I suppose that if I tasted the
ring often enough, it would dissolve, go away, cease to exist."

"Your obsession with jewelry," he said. "You always made
me take off my wristwatch when we made love."

"Yes."

"I tried to make something symbolic out of that. That you
wanted to stop time—wanted to make the love endless."

"That's you," she said. "You and your gift for ignoring the
obvious—that I simply didn't want to be scratched up." She
looked down at her hands. "Time was *your* problem. Don't

forget how often you reminded me about the difference in our ages."

"Twenty-one years," he said. "You don't catch up."

She looked at him, sidelong, a faint smile turning up one thin corner of her mouth.

"So you finally persuaded me," she said. "You obliged me to think about that discrepancy which seemed to you so terrible—made me think of the prospect of your dying, and me left behind to deal God knows how with your paintings, your insurance policies, your debts. Oh, Lord, all of it. Your poor wife. I trusted your own worst fears."

"But I never wanted you to leave me."

"Oh, really," she said, "what else could you have expected, after all was said and done? You harped on it so, reminding me I was so damned young."

"You were damned desirable."

"No," she said. "That was more symptom than cause—the desirability. It was youth you wanted, needed. God knows why that's desirable; it's so ignorant and artless."

"And I was just beginning to do good work. I needed someone to share it with."

"I was starting my own good work," she said.

"I knew you were."

"The bloody hell you did. It never crossed your mind. Or only to the extent that you fancied yourself a Svengali, or a Pygmalion." She pushed back his sleeve to read the time. "I really do have to get to that dinner."

"I could see you tomorrow," he said.

She hesitated—turning him in her mind, he thought.

"Not tomorrow; tomorrow's impossible."

"Later tonight?"

"Where is this flat you've taken?" She rummaged through her purse, producing a gold pen and a small notepad. "I ought to see if your tastes have improved with age; I never understood how a painter could have such dismal color sense."

* * *

When he returned to the apartment he searched among his
books to find the only one of hers he was sure he had brought
with him. It was her first, or her second—he didn't know
which; he had bought it in Chicago, carried it with him to a
symposium at the Art Institute school, sat with it on the table
in front of him. Her picture watched him from the back of
the jacket—the younger, pretty face with its shrewd mouth
and clear eyes, calmly calculating. Somehow he had lost the
thread of the meeting's discussion; a friend nudged him,
chided him. Had he ever gone on to read the book? He
opened it now to the first chapter:

> All she wanted from the world was a sense of the femaleness
> of eternity, of being more than simply a moment to be
> enjoyed, or not enjoyed, by a man.

It was familiar, that opening sentence. He could not be
sure if he had actually read it, or if perhaps he had heard her
say something like it, or if it was only that he imagined
himself to be foremost among the men who had "enjoyed"
her. After she left him in Boston, when he tried to picture
her with a new lover, he could not. They had shared such
intimacies, the possibility of her repeating them with other
men seemed indecent. Once, on a Valentine's Day, she gave
him a card she had made from rice paper and colored inks.
The center of the card was a delicate image he could not at
first identify—a flower, he thought, or the paw print of some
rare creature she had found in a Larousse or a field guide.
Finally he had been obliged to ask her.
"Do you like it?" she said. "Does it please you?"
"It's beautiful."
She had smiled and kissed him. "I'm surprised at you," she
said. "It's the impression of a nipple—mine, actually. I used
one of those felt pads for the inking; then I pressed the paper
against my left breast. Nearest the heart. I didn't get it quite
right the first time; I used too much pressure and lost a lot of
the detail."

Now he remembered the card vividly: the image both ex-
otic and erotic. He had treasured it, kept it for years afterward. Eventually, in a move from one house to another, it
was lost.

But what had she said, later that Valentine's Day?

"You didn't think I had the imagination for such a thing,
did you? You never gave me that much credit."

He closed the book and went to get himself a drink. He
could not merely sit. He opened the Martell he had taken
care to unpack among the first of his possessions—after the
Giacometti, but before the books—to wait splendidly. If she
did not come, if he drank too much cognac and went to sleep,
then it would be his most relaxed evening since the Grand
Exhibition. A consolation of sorts, something to keep his
mind away from work.

"I was starting my own good work," she had reminded him.

And it was true: he had begrudged it. Nights when he could
not fall asleep, he blamed her, getting up and going to the
tiny second bedroom she had arranged as a study, standing
accusingly in the doorway until she turned away from the
typewriter with a look that was distant, mildly perplexed.
"What?" she said. "You know I can't sleep in that damned
bed alone," he said. Or else: "Are you going to hammer on
that thing all night?" Something like that. Even now it was
not clear to him why he could not have said, simply, "I want
you." Instead, always it was a question of ego: the assertion of
his, the belittling of hers.

It was what had unsettled him about the Exhibition—how
the show gathered all his pretensions into a single focus.
Walking through the white rooms while the last paintings
were mounted—after nearly a month of coming to terms with
works he had never expected to see again, borrowed from
owners whose names had become fictions—his whole productive life was before his eyes at once. At one point he had
persuaded himself the task was impossible, that no one could
manipulate and organize his career from its beginnings to a

present he feared was its end. But paintings he had privately
disavowed, experiments he had fled from, obsessions and pre-
occupations out of whose grip he had wrenched himself—
here they all were, apparently inescapable and damning.
In a fashion he could not put into words, the paintings
uncovered his ego; a wise critic would surely comprehend
him, and it was ironic that he could neither comprehend himself nor bring to his own work a coherent critical
wisdom.

Now his personal life seemed to insist a similar comprehen-
sion. Out of the loves and infatuations and sexual partnerings
of the uneasy days when marriage had begun to seem an
impediment in the way of every desire, he could not have
thought this talented woman to be so strong an organizing
principle, and as he sipped brandy from a water glass—he had
found only one of the two snifters he owned, and that was for
her—scenes from his years with her came to mind and glided
away. "You make me sing like silk," she had said once, lying
naked, eyes closed while he caressed her, and even as she said
it he had thought: No, something more substantial, not silk
but clay, and that she could not come to life without the
genius of his hands. Pygmalion indeed. "Sometimes I pant for
you," she said one winter day after furious loving, the snow
outside the apartment windows driven by an east wind, all
traffic halted, all other lives buried.

Once they had stood together on a street in Cambridge
while a motorcade swept past. From a black limousine with
open windows John Kennedy waved, smiled—at them, certainly—and they had hugged each other, thinking themselves
favored. When Kennedy was elected, they imagined they
shared something of destiny. Now he saw that it was more
than destiny—or celebrity or youth or wealth—but promise
not only political. Talisman, perhaps. Because she was the
cynical one, she was to say to him in the aftermath of an
argument that Kennedy was too good to be true, just as living
together was too good. Long after, when they had been apart

for months, she would have scoffed to know how he had wept
over the man's murder; she would have said, "What did you
expect?" Not talisman. Omen. Now when he traveled between America and Europe he missed the old name of the
airport: Idlewild. He shook his head at his perverse sentimentality. Tomorrow, again, she would be gone. All this was
mere surprise, the pleasure of strangers in a foreign land seeing
a familiar face. Tomorrow—one tomorrow or another—an
icy wind would drive mists of snow into the cracks between
the city's paving stones; the open space of the Raadhusplads
would become a weave of delicate white threads against a
cold red fabric. And tonight he put another splash of the
Martell into his glass to help collect himself.

By the time he heard the noise of the outside door he was
giddy from drink, and the sound of his name echoing in the
downstairs hallway provoked a shiver of relief. He waited on
the landing as she climbed the narrow staircase.
    "I thought you might stay away," he said.
    She let him take her hand. "Simple curiosity," she said.
    "I could only find one real snifter. I saved it for you."
    "You remember how I prize the form of things," she said.
    While he poured the cognac she sat under the window that
looked onto the Gothersgade.
    "How was your dinner?"
    "Not unpleasant," she said. "Nice people, a good deal of
praising and toasting that began to make me uncomfortable."
She accepted the drink from him. "But it was odd, how you
intruded between courses and during the after-dinner elo-
quences. It's staggering how much I remember of our time.
When I first saw you at the theater . . . I recognized you, of
course, but really you looked quite different. Part of it was
that you'd shaved the beard—I suppose because it betrayed
you with gray hair and you got tired of confronting it—and
part of it was simple forgetting. I'm fascinated by how the

familiar self slowly reappears in people we haven't seen for a long time. A metamorphosis. Daphne out of her tree."

She looked into the circle of cognac and sipped—a slow, pensive movement. Her eyes engaged his over the crystal rim.

"I see you reappearing too," he said.

"Heaven forbid," she said. "Out of my tree indeed." She set the glass aside. "Might I be given the tour?"

"There isn't much to see. This room, one bedroom, a small kitchen."

"And a bath?"

"I share it."

She was before the mirror and took down the Giacometti, turning it, frowning over it; finally she set it back on the mantel.

"It's gorgeous," she said. "The way he makes the human body vulnerable and rugged at the same time."

"It was a present. A friend in New York."

"She has taste."

"Yes."

"But you like it, too? You don't display it out of sentiment only?"

"Of course not. What you said: the way he sees the extremes of the body—the beauty, the coarseness."

"But genderless," she finished. She sat loosely in the brocade chair. "I used to wonder why you weren't a sculptor, some latter-day Rodin in a studio cluttered with statues and goose-pimpled models."

"I tried it, back in those days."

"Yes, the maquettes," she said. "I remember those awful pornographic things you did—and claimed they were you and me."

"But they were."

"Only in your wildest fancies." She turned the glass in her hands. "Where will you work while you're in Copenhagen? Is there a studio? Upstairs? Close by?"

"None of the above," he said. "I'm here purely for escape."

He saw her perplexity. "How can you 'escape' from work like yours? It isn't as if you were a factory hand, packing the wife and kids into the caravan for a holiday. Everything is in your head; you can't erase it by tying your hands."

"The head's pretty useless right now."

"Nonsense."

"Oh, I still have ideas, notions, plans; I just don't seem able to nurture them. Or I forget whatever the hell it was I had in mind."

"Burnout, I suppose," she said.

"Whatever that is."

"I don't mean to rag you for not working, but I know what a genius you were at excusing laziness. As if you wanted posterity to feel remorse for the work you didn't do. Still, I'm not unsympathetic, really."

She stopped, seemed to reach for a cigarette then change her mind.

"A few years ago *I* went through an arid time," she said. "It was tied up with life's ordinariness. One always wishes for a pure literary existence—as if one's work could be divorced from sleeping and eating and brushing the teeth. At any rate, I had rather a bad go of it."

She smiled sheepishly at him. "I'd sit at the typewriter, staring at the page I'd just rolled in, and I'd start to shake. I'd be positively scared. Something like your old anxiety thing, I imagine.

"Or I'd open my eyes in the morning and lie in that delectable land between dreaming and waking, and whole scenes would come—characters, dialogue, motives and intentions. 'My God,' I'd think, 'what a wonderful plan,' and all in an instant it would vanish—people, place, and thing totally gone as if I'd never imagined them. The rest of the morning I'd sit by the window with one of those lined stationer's pads in my lap; by the time I was hungry, all I'd done on the pad was write my initials a thousand times."

"What was happening then? In your life."

She held her glass against the light. The color of the brandy made a small glow on her forehead.

"It really is better from a snifter, isn't it?"

"You won't say?" he prompted.

"My secret," she said. "Though the pattern of most secret-keeping is that in the end one tells all. Anyway, I passed through that dark time of not being able to write anything more pressing than a note to the milkman. As they say: I persevered."

He waited.

"Forgive me," she said. "Probably I only want to reverse our old roles, so that I can sit across from you and give you advice about the way the artist's life should be lived."

"I don't mind," he said.

"I saw a film once, on television—a reunion of Stravinsky with your friend Giacometti, in Paris. Not long after the first time I went to England, I think. Did you see it?"

"No."

"Here were these two old men talking, each one sketching the other, and when the program was done we were shown what they'd drawn. Both the sketches were astonishingly good. I'd have expected that from Giacometti. But Stravinsky . . . My word, I thought, he could probably have done anything he wanted with his life. And then I thought of those famous photographs of Picasso making art from the bones of the fish he'd just had for supper . . ."

"Genius," he said.

"Yes, I keep hearing talk about 'genius.' It always seems a frantic stumbling in the dark."

"You have to account for things," he said.

Now she did find a cigarette and lighted it carefully. Out of her purse she produced a small silver box and opened it—an ashtray—on the window ledge beside her.

"I remember your saying to me once: 'I never worry about losing an idea, because two others always take its place.' Then you said: 'Ideas are miracles.' "

"And now I'm contradicting myself?"

"Don't be defensive." She looked both amused and concerned. "I'm just an old lover, not the critic from *The Times.*"

"I suppose it has something to do with being off-balance at seeing you again," he said. "And you've changed—you're a woman now."

"I always was."

"A wiser one, I mean."

"That puts you off? A flicker of wisdom in the weaker sex?"

"Besides, you're the famous one," he said. "Respected. Praised. Hollywood making movies out of your books. Handsome young men pursuing you . . ."

"Stop that," she said. "I've not had many men in my life these last few years." She spoke softly—the statement so private he could hardly hear her. Whatever hurt he had touched, the room swam with it.

"I can't believe—"

"I know. I'm so personable, I'm so attractive, I've never prized myself highly enough. My God, I remember your telling me those things when I was feeling like the ugly duckling who hadn't yet got the news of swan-hood. But that was a time—yes, I really understood—when you loved me as best you knew how, and I welcomed all those lies. But not now, please."

"Listen," he said. He reached out to her—from sympathy or love, he couldn't tell which—but she pushed his hands away.

"You mayn't touch me," she said.

"I want to."

Then he was kneeling in front of her; he kissed her eyes, her mouth, amazed that she kissed back. He stroked her coarse hair.

"O dear man," she said, "please think what you're doing. You play on all my old weakness for you—all my fretfulness for your nightmares and frustrations." She put her hands to his face. "Hell and damn," she said. "I'm not strong enough.

When we first talked—in the restaurant—I wasn't much stirred by you. I thought: Look how old he really is. I thought: Christ, he was right all along. And then I thought you'd grown smug, complacent about how far you'd succeeded. Now I see something worse—pathetic. A kind of hollowing-out."

He held her hands and kissed them. "I've felt like that," he said.

"And so have I. Except it used to be only a pose with you —a snare for women who rather believed it was noble to inspire an artist by sleeping with him."

"You're too hard on me."

"I thought I'd got off you for good," she said. "And I had; I'd got off you and every other likely man whose path crossed mine. I'd loved you and been loved back, I'd hated you and gotten away, I'd turned you into words and made money off you. There was nothing else I needed from you." She caught at his wrists and drew him to his feet. "But have it your way," she said. "Take me to bed."

In his first excitement over her—the dizziness, the sweet taste in his mouth—he might have been coaxed to think he was a young man, renewed, rekindled. And of her: that whatever grudge she might have carried over the years was as easily overcome as any other frail excuse.

"Wait," she said. "No." He had undone the first button of her blouse. "I'll do you."

Then she undressed him, kissing and whispering, until he was naked for her. He sat on the edge of the bed and let go his restraint. Or almost let go, for by keeping her clothes on she had made him self-conscious in front of her, and he felt awkward to be naked.

"Let me," he said, and he hurried to remove her clothing in turn—but she would not let him take off the blouse.

"I don't want you to touch me there," she said.

He held her, tried to read her face in the lamplight.

"No," she said. "Don't look at me."

She slid off the bed and went to the dresser, where she had laid her purse. He thought she was after a smoke. Instead she stood, motionless, with her back toward him.

"Please," he said.

She unfastened the buttons and turned to face him, slipping the blouse off her shoulders to the floor. Her eyes glistened.

"There," she said, "you see." She came to him, stood naked in front of him. "You see what's left of me."

He sat on the edge of the bed and held her and pressed the side of his face against her bare stomach. "Oh, love," he said.

He felt her sigh, as if she were letting go of herself.

"Oh, my poor love," he said again.

She raised his head and held it against her scarred chest. "Isn't it dreadful," she said. "They lopped me off like someone in a book for the butcher's children."

"When?"

"Five years ago; and two years ago. They let me do it twice, to get it right." She hugged him, hard. "Fearful symmetry. I swore I'd never again let a man see me."

"Don't," he said. He could only hold her. "Don't."

"I know; by now I should've come to terms with it, and mostly I have." She sat beside him, her cheek against his shoulder. "You," she said; "you never could let me keep my clothes on."

"Did you think you'd frighten me away?"

"I didn't know," she said. "I don't know anything—whether I still qualify as a woman; why a man would want to look at me, touch me; what's going to happen next."

He kissed her forehead, her eyes, her mouth. He traced with his fingertips the muscles of her neck to where they met the breastbone and formed the delicate hollow cup. When he tried to move his hand lower, she caught it and held it fast.

"You have such lovely skin," he said.

She was watching his face intently, and he looked up to meet her gaze.

"You can't take your eyes away, can you?" she said. "You're fascinated."

He shivered. "It doesn't make me feel any different about you." Yet even as he said the words, he was not sure of them.

"Sweet liar," she said.

"All right, I don't know how to react," he said. "That's the truth."

"I've wished I could blame someone, blame something. I wish I could account for it," she said. "I used to think I was being punished for my vanity. That it was because when I was twenty I used to shriek at my poor mirror: 'Oh, why didn't God give me a figure?' You pay the price for that sort of thing, I decided. It's like the pitiless justice you get in the fairy tales, or in the old Greek myths. You get turned into the thing you most despised, and you don't get second chances."

She drew his hands to her mouth and kissed his fingers.

"Or the gods are just enough hard of hearing so that they garble your wish, or so distracted—like good fathers—that they don't listen all the way to the end." She was weeping, and trying very hard not to. It had been all these years since he had seen her cry, and never over anything more important than whether or not he loved her. Now that love was no longer the issue—they were perhaps friends, or colleagues of a sort—the tears seemed crucial. Twenty years earlier he could have embraced her, touched her. The tears would have stopped; the woman would have pressed against him, returning the touching, and then they would be making love.

He freed one of his hands and stroked the nape of her neck.

"Oh, I know." She shook her head out from under his hand. "All the strategies for taking one's mind away from the immediate problem. Distractions, deceptions, nice obstructions. More art."

"You aren't any easier to distract than ever."

She lay against the pillows and pulled him to her. "I didn't mean the distractions no longer worked," she said. "I only meant that I've got more conscious of them." She put her hand down to him. "May we do it now?"

He knelt over her, bowed toward her.

"But no; just one second." She caught his left hand. "This damned watch of yours."

Only once, when he kissed the two fierce scars that slanted like Oriental brushstrokes across her chest, did she speak during lovemaking. "Poor baby," she said. "I remember how you liked to kiss my nipples."

Afterward they lay entwined, comfortable. He marveled that the passion—the word startled him—of his sixties seemed no less consuming than the ardor of his forties. And no less joyous.

"How will you remember me? I wonder," she said.

"Like this," he said. He kissed her throat, nuzzled her. "Wise and brave, and always short with me."

"No, I mean what will you *do* to remember me?"

His mind fluttered over answers. He wanted not to be trivial or flippant again. Or foolish.

"We could be together," he said. "The question needn't come up."

"I'm serious," she said.

"Then don't be. It isn't as if we weren't going to see each other again."

"But suppose we weren't."

"No," he said, "I won't rise to hypothetical cases."

Some years after his living with her—he had read a long interview with her in a magazine, and his sense of having lost her was roused—he wrote her a letter, addressed in care of her publisher. *One of my worst fears,* he had written as a postscript, *is that I will be dying, and no one will know where to find you.* She had never answered the letter.

"You used never to rise to real cases, either," she said. "The best you ever managed was to confuse them."

"Sometimes it doesn't make any difference, does it?"

"But sometimes it does. If I were writing this as a love

scene in the next novel, could I get away with a cosmetic falsehood?"

"No," he said. "This time I'd recognize us."

"The wisdom of age," she said.

"And the truth is, this is as near to Paradise as I've been in a long time."

She kissed him. "The new Eden. Adam sans beard, and Eve sans tits."

"But it isn't the end of the world."

"Or else it is," she said. "I had an aunt went the way I'm going, a piece at a time, continually hearing the this-time-we-got-it-all fable. They never get it all."

"No faith in science?" he said.

"Of all things? No—unless you mean the faith that science will carry off all of us before it carries off any one of us."

"Not exactly."

"I thought not. Though I mustn't deceive you: science brought me the only man I'm not ashamed to undress for. A medical type—the chief radiologist at my clinic. Not a surprising affair; I see him often enough."

"This is in England?"

"No. Oh, God, no. I love the English. But trust myself to their medical system? I'm far from suicidal."

"So you were where? Back in the States?"

"Stanford. As it happened, I'd gone out there, all innocent —I mean, I didn't know anything was wrong with me— simply to live for a while. A friend of mine had a house in the Portola Valley; I was working on the new book."

She leaned her chin on her knees.

"Anyway, one morning in the shower I found this lump, just like the women's-magazine scenario. I don't suppose it was actually very big, but in my terrified cosmology it felt like a tenth planet. So off I ran: tests, X-rays, mammograms—all that vocabulary of woman as guinea pig.

"And I met Brendan, who really knew his job and was easy to talk to. Much easier than the doctors who chivvied me in

and out of major and minor surgeries. I could ask Brendan
questions, and he'd give me answers. It's ignorance, you
know, makes us afraid."

"I know," he said.

"I remember I said to him: 'How do we know all these X-
rays won't make the cancer worse?' You read about that in
the popular magazines. D'you know what he told me?

"That when he was head of radiology at a private hospital
in the Bay area, he realized nobody had the slightest idea how
much radiation was enough in breast-tumor cases. Everybody
thought too high a level was bad, but nobody knew how much
was too much." She put her hands over her eyes. "My God,"
she said, "when you think how delicate we are . . .

"So Brendan set out to discover how much was enough. He
couldn't just do it by trial and error; he had to find a reason-
able facsimile of the female breast—papier-mâché, or Play-
Doh, or something—without experimenting on all the nice
ladies. You know what he finally used? Unsliced bacon and
black olives. All he had to do was adjust the radiation so a
film reader could discriminate the pit from the flesh of the
olive in its setting of bacon."

She seemed to have begun crying again. He reached out to
her, drew her against him and held her. "Imagination," she
said. Her body shook with dry sobs. "Bloody wonderful imagination."

"What can I do?" he said.

"Nothing. Only I remember thinking about the coincidences of time: here was my mother putting me into a training
bra, and out in California this darling man was inventing a
cancerous breast."

He embraced her. "Stay with me," he said.

She shook her head. Strands of her dark hair lay across his
mouth.

"Please. At least stay the night."

She pushed herself away from him, kneeling, hugging herself. "I can't. I've got a television thing, and a luncheon, and

some kind of party at the translator's house later in the day.
And then the charter to catch. Tomorrow's to be an ordeal; I
wish I could chuck it."

"Please."

She bowed her head, dropped her hands to stroke his hips
—idly, he thought, like a cat probing a blanket.

"All right. But you have to get me out of here early. Word
of honor; I oughtn't to stand any of these people up." She
leaned to kiss his eyes. "A one-nighter," she said. "That's all
this is."

"We'll see," he said.

"And this isn't Paradise," she said. "You're not to become
mawkish about us."

He held her. Surveying their two bodies in this bed, he was
fascinated by how thin they both were. "We're both fragile,"
he said. He caressed her throat, her shoulder, let his fingers
move lightly along the scar lines on her ravaged chest. He
felt the intake of her breath. The scars had a different texture
from the surrounding flesh—smooth, taut. He bowed his
head to kiss them. She cradled his head against her; he could
feel her trembling, hear her heart beating.

"Are you mostly content?" he said finally. "With your
work, your books? Has it all come out pretty much as you
wanted?"

She sighed—ruefully, he thought. "Some of my daydreams
came gloriously true," she said. "Others are as far off—remote
—as they ever were. I've made money, even where the tax
laws are crushing. I've had enough fame, I expect; more might
have killed me some other way. I've said a lot of the things I
wanted to say when I knew you, only at the time I was stifled
by your long shadow." She stopped. "Again you have the
most peculiar smile on your face," she said. "You do make me
feel quite caught out. What is it I've said?"

"In the years we lived together, we never talked this much
about ourselves."

"Because we were too simpleminded to realize what a rich

quantity we amounted to. I always thought we made love too much; it stole time from philosophy." She reached out to press his hands with hers. "Not to deprecate this night," she said. "I'd not trade it back."

" 'Enough' fame, you said."

"Which means *you* still believe there's *never* enough. I'm not persuaded. Sometimes even a little is too much—the way it fills time and space—and I resent it. Once in London I actually wore a blond wig and dark glasses with rhinestone frames. I felt not so much admired as hunted. They've never got me back on the BBC, I'll tell you."

"Are we talking about fame or celebrity?"

She shrugged. "All right. The worst thing I can say about fame-as-fame is that the fantasy of one day being able to trade a piece of my writing for a Henry Moore still hasn't come true. Not to slight you—but Moore . . . I think in my middle age I've been much more deeply drawn into his natural world, his metaphors. It isn't only that so many of his women have holes where there ought to be breasts, but that his figures, human or not, seem married to the earth; they aren't afraid of the association. I like that. It soothes me."

"You could *buy* a sculpture, couldn't you?"

"I suppose. I imagine there's money enough. But would you feel as happy about your little Giacometti if you'd bought it? I'd rather earn such a thing—trade talent for talent. I ought to have lived in some kind of prehistory, a universe of barter. No money, no plastic." She brushed several strands of hair away from his forehead. "And you? Has the world turned out for you?"

"You know all that."

"Only that you seem to think an artist has to retire at sixty-five."

"If he's forced to it."

"You're so damned pretentious about time," she said. "You were always proud of looking youthful; you used to encourage people—women—to guess your age because you knew they'd guess low. Here . . ." She left him and came back with the gold pen. Beside him in bed, she took his left wrist and drew a watch face on the top of it, traced two lines around the wrist for the strap—taking pains to draw in the buckle. "You've just enough leftover farmer tan for me to trace."

"Couldn't you make it an expansion band?"

"Piss off," she said. "Make allowance for persons of minimal talent. What time would you like it to be?"

"Whatever it is right now."

She consulted his watch on the bedside table and copied its hands onto him. "Why could you never be as vain about your talent as you were about your boyish appearance?" she said. "It might have saved us from this claptrap about your creative juices drying up."

"Maybe I've needed someone to drive me," he said.

"I'll drive you," she said. "To drink and awful excess." She put aside the pen and flung herself against him, wrestling and pummeling with such energy he wasn't sure whether she was being playful or angry. At first he was afraid of being hurt— I'm an old man, he wanted to say—and then he was laughing, helpless to ward her off. Finally she rested against him.

"I surrender," he said.

She kissed his eyes. "May we do love again? Isn't it still true about older men—their patience, their endurance?"

"I can't answer that. You've made me young."

"And you've made me whole," she said. "A beautiful lie makes beautiful the thing lied about."

He woke up once in the middle of the night. When he opened his eyes in the dark, all the happenings of the day— settling the apartment, walking through the city, trying to attend the ballet—slowly led to the fact of the woman he lay with. The room smelled of loving, of sweat and perfume and heavy sexual humidity. Roses and low tide, she had said to him, once when they had driven to the Cape and slept together in an old brass bed, in a room that sighed with ocean. He was on his back; she lay on top of him with her head nested under his chin, her slender arms around his neck, threaded into the space between his shoulders and the pillow.

Loving. He had learned the odor of it in the Juárez his army comrades, true to their promise, took him to. In a smoky cantina one of them, a gangling youngster who had rough-necked in a West Texas oil field, instructed him—sent him to bed with a woman scarcely old enough to have left her parents. She was small, sparrow-boned, with a child's delicate features; her English was no more fluent than his Spanish. They helped each other undress. She had seemed to know it was his first time, and dealt with him patiently. *"Muy bonito,"* she kept saying. Afterward, when she had sponged herself at the bidet in one corner of the small room, she came back to the bed and he held her, kissing her throat, her breasts. The only light in the room was from a single candle, and he was conscious of a silver crucifix hanging above the bed. Was that as close as he had been to a "religious" experience? Her hands caressed his back; her hard nipples were sweet under his tongue.

When he drew away from her, he saw the reason for the sweetness: a tiny seed pearl of milk at the tip of one breast. It surprised him; he felt fear—or shame—as if he had violated a law, committed a sacrilege. *"Leche,"* he said, meaning it as both question and apology. She had smiled shyly. Then he learned, half from words, half from gestures, how she had recently given birth, how the man was to be her husband, how she was whoring in this border town to put together a dowry. Would he like to see the child? Would he like to enter her again? No, he told her. No, *gracias.* The memory was like a dream.

When he woke again, he was alone. The light that came in through the small windows was flat and colorless. The linens beside him and over him had no warmth, neither of her nor of himself, as if they had held nothing alive. He sat

up. He felt stiff—the muscles of his upper back shuddered
in a spasm that was close to pain, and he consciously
straightened himself. Age. Dying. One came to terms with it;
one dealt with it, lived in spite of it. As she had, apparently.
"Remission," she had said, just before they slept. The word
carried the sense of a dispensation, a permission to survive;
"not necessarily renewable," she added.

He wondered if she could recall his touching her breasts
when he first loved her. Was memory physical? Or was it
intellectual, an abstraction, for words—hers, surely—to
make as sensual as possible? Perhaps the pleasure of here and
now replaced the old memories, as he had once persuaded
himself that making love to her obliterated all her past lovers.
Anyway, where was she? It pleased him—flattered him—to
think of her waiting to be taken to breakfast. Yet when he
went out into the living room where they had drunk brandy
the night before, she was truly gone. On the mantel, under
its Giacometti paperweight, was a sheaf of lined notebook
paper, each page covered with her left-handed scrawl:

It's four in the morning. It isn't that I can't sleep, but
that I won't—it's a luxury I haven't time for. I shouldn't
cater to you by saying how happy I feel, how relaxed I am
—more than in months, truly—and yet it's selfish to keep
the happiness to myself. There's no place for selfishness, is
there, in a life genuinely lived; selfishness is for lives eked
out, as by landlords afraid to be stolen from. I never again
want a life of that sort. So. You make me happy. Yes, you
do. It doesn't of course atone for the past; you needn't as
you read this imagine (in your male vanity) that you are
forgiven your trespasses for being magnanimous to someone
whose weakness you discovered on just the right day—
that's too easy, and doesn't constitute forgiveness in anyone's religion. You only make me happy—have made me
happy. No implications for the future. None.

How odd to be sitting in your parlor. How odd to be
writing a note—this perverse billet-doux—to a man pres-

ently snoring in a bed I've only just now got up from.
Though it's the sort of thing that used to happen all the
time. You, you "visual artist," obliging yourself to work in
the daylight, while I worked by night—batlike and incom-
petent (!) by day. "Conniving over the midnight oil," you
used to say, chastising me. Such irreconcilable differences:
painters who must love by night, and writers perfectly will-
ing to love at any hour. O poor visual artists!

So. I am up, and dawn is not rosy-fingered because the
rain is raining everywhere. Autumn. Another summer
gone; my "lover" asleep in the next room. Familiar scenes
for us both. I hope other women have reminded you how
vulnerable you are in your sleeping—mouth slack, throat
bared to a jealous knife, et cetera. In truth, this morning I
thought you touching—affecting. I wanted to kiss that im-
becile mouth, say a prayer to the gods of paint and palette
to inspire you, save you from your imagined despairs. Stop
posing romantically. Oh please do stop.

I want you to remember me. I've precious small faith in
the books I've written—Who will read between the lines
and say: "There she was, there she is. She set herself down
better than she knew." We are hardly ever seen to be writing ourselves. We always hope we've scribbled our own
immortality, but the hope is vain and I no longer hug it.

I used to have charms against mortality. I used even to
believe—my modified, sophomore Platonism—that the
universe held a finite number of souls—that the few billion
of us on Earth died and were reborn over and over. It
seemed efficient. It seemed the sort of plan a beneficent
God with a lot of other matters at hand might have pre-
ferred. How nice, I thought, to know that when you died
you could expect to return to the living. It didn't matter
that one's memory was erased in the process; that was price
small enough, and who wanted to look back, anyway? But
no Heaven and no Hell—that mattered.

Now I know how prolific Nature is—wasteful, prodigal,
extravagant—how infinitely productive. That's what ge-

nius is. What's efficiency to God? Nature will try anything.
Look at evolution. Look at the stars. Look at damned cancer.

The good news is: Nothing is ever finished, and nothing
is ever enough—and so you cannot stop being a painter,
though you think you've no pictures left, and I cannot stop
being a writer, though I've no time left. I'm not sentimental. I don't imagine how I might have taught you that
lesson—staying with you, surviving your failure of love—
and I don't regret not trying. But now I am come to selfishness, saying like a cranky prophet that I expect you to make
up for ignoring me all this time. It can't hurt you to attend
to me; like everything else, our attentions are inexhaust-
ible.

I can't offer you the same. In April, when England's
excessive green will begin to mean spring, I'll be back in
California with Brendan, having his comfort by night and
his knowledge by day. I expect our paths—yours and mine
—won't cross again. You should keep reading my books.
You should go to the cinema, even if what you see is not
about yourself. You should remember, always remember, to
be extravagant.

The last page she had signed with her initial.

For a time he stood at the window, the sheets of scribbled
notepaper tight in his hands. The weather had turned worse
—the street below his window grayed by fog, the horizon
beyond the Nikolai Kirke shrouded in mists that rendered sky
indistinguishable from earth. Rain was falling, hard, the drops
streaming down the window. At the sill, he noticed, water
was seeping in; the gold-flecked wallpaper under the window
was stained brown from earlier storms—years of them, probably—and stood away from the plaster underneath in two
parallel bubbles.

Later, when he arrived in the lobby of the Palace he found
she was no longer there—she had checked out "very early,"
the clerk told him—and though he tried to telephone the

airport, he had difficulty first with the receiver and then with the operator, whose English was unexpectedly poor.

He crossed the street and went into a restaurant on the Raadhusplads for breakfast—something American, unthinkable in the nineteen-forties. Waiting, he noticed the pale-blue outline of the watch drawn on his wrist; he dabbed at it, idly, with a finger of his right hand. At a table nearby, a blonde young woman opened her blouse to suckle the infant in her lap. For just a moment before the child found it, he saw the full breast, the swollen nipple, and when the young mother smiled at him he realized she had caught him staring.

The Eventual Nuclear Destruction of Cheyenne, Wyoming

W hat impressed Marshall Eames about Wyoming was the sense that it existed outside ordinary space and time. There was no place like it; there never had been any place like it. Driving cross-country from east to west, leaving behind the Atlantic Coast of white beaches and gray cottages, of girls lanky and windburned and strong enough to sail their own boats, he had felt a gathering strangeness, as if he were a foreigner, an immigrant from a land on the far side of that familiar ocean horizon. And in fact, curiously, he was a foreigner. All of America—the high places of the Berkshires and Catskills, the vineyards of western New York, the expanse of Ohio and Indiana and Illinois where the late-spring air was gritty with blown soil that turned the sunsets red, the unimaginable sweep of the Great Plains—all of it was novel and unexpected and like a land only a spinner of stories could have devised. There was so much of it; it was so open; it had, this land, so much vulnerable sky.

The sky had brought him here. He was on his way to California—had been for nearly four months—making the journey in his white Chevy van by patient stages, one job at a time. He worked for the Cem-Tech corporation, a company whose workers believed there was nothing they could not build out of poured concrete. He had helped construct petroleum storage tanks along the Hudson River, grain elevators near Champaign, Illinois, and Hastings, Nebraska, and now he was part of the crews setting missile silos outside Cheyenne. Whenever he heard of a Cem-Tech job commencing to the west, he signed up for it. He calculated that by the end of the year he would be in California, though he was in no hurry. He was still twenty-four. He had no steady girl to complicate his life, felt no obligation to his parents, in Marblehead, and he held one good-pay job after another at a time when work was scarce. If he didn't get to the Coast by the end of next year—that was fine. Each new job site meant that many more payments on the van, and at the rate he was going the bank would be off his back by the time he turned twenty-six. Wyoming was no state where he wanted to spend the rest of his days, but it wasn't treating him badly, was it?

He was living not far from the missile site's eastern edge, on a gravel road a few miles out of Hillsdale, in a solitude that satisfied him. He had a sound system as good as he could afford, and a collection of cassette tapes packed in two cardboard boxes that had held, respectively, a Seth Thomas ship's clock and a barometer. At the end of the workday, when he had showered at the site and perhaps stopped for one beer on the way home, he liked nothing better than to cook up a little bacon for a bacon-and-cheese sandwich on bakery bread, and to sprawl on the bunk he had built behind the driver's seat to listen to music as loud as he wanted.

Even when he worked double shifts—and sometimes he stayed on the job twenty-four hours, because the foreman trusted him and the extra money was hard to turn down—he had the feeling that his life was beginning to make good sense, that he had a future as well as a present. Getting up at five in the morning, driving to the site through green plains already beginning to imitate the light and shadow of the mountains that lay west of here, he felt privileged and singular. Once at the site and deeply involved in the work— setting reinforcing bars in the wide trenches the forms made, watching the rivers of concrete like a flood tide rising relentlessly to crest, drawing up the forms to contain the next pouring—he was one of a team. Ants, he had thought when he first arrived on the job. The excavated earth swarmed with men as numerous and purposeful as ants; the swarming appeared chaotic, but every man knew his mission. Marshall felt he had the best of two worlds, one of solitude, the other of comradeship.

It was only after work, when he was unwinding, having a drink or two, that he gave any thought to the nature of his job. Doing it, involved in it, he had no doubts. The people who haunted the roads leading to the site—people with signboards, people whose eyes seemed to Marshall to be accusing him of some crime he knew he was not committing—they were only one more element of an unfamiliar landscape. Once a rock had struck the side of his van; he stopped and jumped out to confront the thrower. She was an older woman—in her fifties, he guessed—and she stood defiantly as he charged toward her. Facing her, he could hardly think what to say. He wanted her to be a man, so he could strike at her, or younger, so he could wither her with sarcasm and profanity. He wanted to say: Damn it, lady, we're saving your life here. Finally, all he said was

"Don't do that again."

And then he said:

"Please."

He was never much for talk. Words made him feel awkward, perhaps because he was afraid he might admit to loneliness. He was too old for sentimentality toward his parents, and still too young to depend on a woman, yet in some part of himself resided a weakness. The lady and her mute defiance touched that weakness, so he was not surprised on that Friday to find himself making plans for Saturday-night drinking with Harold Gance.

"Not like that weekend in Oklahoma City," Marshall said. "Just a few beers."

"Sure enough," Harold said.

"There's a couple of things I wouldn't mind talking about."

Harold had wiped sweat from his face with a shirt sleeve. "You bet," he said.

When he arrived at the roadhouse, Marshall bought a pitcher of beer and located Harold at a crowded table in the back. He raised the pitcher; Harold saw him and waved. Every other face at the table was unfamiliar.

"Here's my buddy Marshall," Harold said. "We worked a couple of places together—most stupidly back in Hastings, where the slip foreman tried to get us both killed in a lightning storm."

"Hello," Marshall said.

"This is my current best girl, Mary Kay—you probably heard about her famous lipstick and face powder—and this is Carl Miller and his wife, Bonnie, who are honest-to-Pete natives of this state."

"Drag over that other table, honey," said Bonnie, "and sit by me."

"Thanks." He pushed the two tables together and sat. "This is the first night out I've had in a couple of weeks."

"You got a lady keeping you in line?"

Marshall shook his head. "Saving money to pay for my van. If the work lasts long enough, I'll be out of debt when I leave here."

"It'll last," Carl Miller said.

"I been here since the very start," Harold said. "I was the third man they hired the day they set up that shed over by Warren Air Base."

"How'd you know to be here?"

"Didn't. I'd driven down from Casper just the day before and heard about it in a bar."

"Damn lucky," Carl said.

"Harold's got a guardian angel," Mary Kay said. "Ain't you, babe?"

"I'll say one thing," Marshall told the table. "I've never in my whole life seen so much concrete as here. And I've seen lots of it."

Heads nodded.

"I had a guy at Warren swear to me that if they put all that mud into an interstate highway, they'd have a four-lane green stamp from Cheyenne to Moscow and back."

"They ought to do it," Mary Kay said. "They could have UPS deliver their atom bombs to the Kremlin mail room and save the air fare."

"Just so's they drove off real fast," Harold said.

"I like the way some of those guys decorate their cement-mixer trucks," Bonnie said. "They get real artistic: American flags, and fancy curlicue designs, and all bright colors, you know?"

"Goddamned trucks," Carl said. "It'd be all right with me if they launched mud trucks at the Russkies, and their jerk drivers inside."

"Carl dropped a hammer he was using to slip forms with," Harold said. "He'd just climbed down to get it when this dipshit driver started pouring."

"Wanted to make you a monument," Marshall said, grinning.

"Wanted to make me goulash," Carl said. He glared at Marshall. "You think it's so Christly funny, you go stand under five yards of mud, why don't you."

"Save it, Carl," Bonnie said. "You lived to tell us about it."

Carl filled his glass from the pitcher. "I lost my g.d. hammer," he said sullenly.

"How many guys you think will die before this job is fin-

ished?" Harold looked around at them. "A serious question,"
he said.

"Who says anybody's going to die?" said Bonnie.

"Oh, yeah," Marshall said, "somebody will, a job as big as
this."

"How many?"

"How many working on it?" Carl asked.

"They say upwards of nine thousand."

"Nine thousand men," Mary Kay said.

Harold punched her shoulder with one knuckle. "You ain't
going to have time to meet all that number," he said.

"You can't shoot a gal for trying." She winked at Bonnie.

"The hell I can't."

"A dozen," Marshall said. "A dozen men'll get killed pouring these silos."

Harold shook his head. "More," he said. "A hell of a lot
more."

"That's right," Carl agreed. "You got so many guys out
there never done this kind of work—never worked with steel,
don't know their ass from their elbow about setting forms.
Plus, most of the work is below ground."

Marshall nodded wisely. "Cave-ins," he said.

"Right, cave-ins. Some of them accidental, some of them
on purpose."

"Nobody's really going to make a cave-in happen." Bonnie
looked at Marshall. "Are they?"

"I get that truck driver down in a hole, I'll show you a
cave-in on purpose."

"Oh Jesus, Carl, you're just talking."

"The hell I am," Carl said. "Quit calling me a liar."

The talk stopped. In the awkward silence Marshall went to
the bar and bought two more pitchers. When he got back to
the table, Harold was saying:

"You got to understand. This is a huge job—all these
crews, all this equipment, everything measured in numbers
bigger than anybody's used to. It's like building the pyramids.

Everybody's falling over everybody else. Everybody thinks they know what's going on. We got nine thousand chiefs and no Indians."

"Me," Marshall said. "I'm an Indian."

"Well you're the only one," Harold said.

"That explains why you drink so much," Bonnie said. "Don't it, Carl?"

"Firewater," Carl said.

Bonnie leaned against Marshall and mussed his hair. "You're cute when you've had a few," she said.

At a quarter to midnight, the five of them were on their way to a dance in Carpenter. They were in Harold's Wagoneer, and a pint of Early Times was making the shuttle between the front and back seats. Harold drove; Mary Kay rode snuggled against him. Marshall and Carl sat in the back with Bonnie between them.

"I've worked all over," Marshall said. He took a swallow from the whiskey bottle and passed it to Bonnie. His eyes watered; he thought probably he hadn't been this drunk in half a year, if ever. "From Massachusetts to here, and in between."

Bonnie handed the bottle to her husband without drinking. "You worked in the Dakotas?"

"Oh yeah, I worked there."

"North or South?"

"Oh yeah," Marshall said. "I worked there."

"Carl had a job in Grand Forks one time," Bonnie said. "Remember, sweetie?"

"Hell, yes. I remember."

"With a natural-gas company," she said. "We were there nearly three years. It was a good job; I thought we'd got out of Wyoming to stay."

"Wasn't that good," Carl said.

"Better than we've had since."

"Until now."

"Where'd that whiskey go?" Marshall said. He took the bottle, drank, and handed it back to Mary Kay. "I drove across North Dakota once, or maybe it was South Dakota. Pheasants—they got pheasants you wouldn't believe. We're talking hundreds and hundreds. I drove across South Dakota and they kept flying up in front of the van, and I kept hitting the damn things."

"Poor birds," Mary Kay said.

"Broke my grille," Marshall said. "Broke a headlight. Cracked my windshield. Hundreds of pheasants."

"That's the end of the hard stuff," Carl said. He cranked the window down and flung the empty bottle into the dark.

"Dead soldier," Harold said.

"You're a native of this place," Marshall said. "Didn't Harold say?"

"Yeah," Bonnie said. "Born right in Cheyenne, twenty-nine years ago next August."

"How you feel about all this?"

"All what? All this missile stuff?"

"Yeah, this missile stuff." He looked at her in the glare of approaching headlights.

She shrugged. "I don't think about it. My folks, they've got two of those Minuteman silos on their ranch, so I was sort of brought up with it—the deterrent thing—and I figure this is just more of the same. Only worse, I guess." She looked down and turned the ring on her left hand. "I reckon it's going to kill all of us anyway, don't you?"

"That's sure something to look forward to."

"I didn't say I was crazy about it."

"You could move someplace else."

"Oh, sure I could," she said. "I could move someplace else. If Carl wanted to move, then I'd move."

"I ain't moving," Carl said. "This is one gorgeous piece of country; if I'm going to die, I'm going to die right here. When they tell me World War Three's started, I'll just drive off into the mountains and look back to Cheyenne for the fireworks."

"And take me," Bonnie said.

"You and your mom and dad and the whole clan," Carl said. "We'll have a Fourth of July picnic."

Bonnie nudged Marshall's ribs.

"See what I told you?" she said.

The dance in Carpenter was at the general store. In it were shelves of groceries and a pop cooler, and on the inside of the front door was a list of the eligible voters in the town; in the back was a large hall, a platform for the band at one end and a bar at the other; between the store and the dance hall was a vestibule, with a popcorn machine on the outside wall, and opposite the popcorn machine the doors into the men's and ladies' rooms. It was half-past midnight when the five of them piled out of the Wagoneer and into the dance, stumbling and laughing and swearing.

"Look at this," Harold said to Marshall. "They got a meat case and everything. If you don't find you an easy girl here, you can buy two pounds of fresh liver on the way out." He whooped; Marshall whooped with him.

"Shush," said Mary Kay. "These are nice country folks. You two behave yourselves."

Marshall stopped to lean against the door that led into the dancing. He made himself stand straight and take a deep breath. He had not drunk so much beer and whiskey in a long time, and he was sure he didn't want to offend Mary Kay or Bonnie or any nice country folks from Carpenter.

"I'm sorry," he said.

Bonnie patted his cheek. "It's okay," she said. "You're forgiven."

Then Harold put a bottle of Bud in his hand and he found himself sitting on a bench, watching the dancers dance. For a time Bonnie was beside him. He remembered her saying:

"Now, don't you worry about us out here. We'll do okay. When you get out to California and get settled, I want you to think about us and how relaxed we all are."

"I will," he told her.

He felt calm. Whatever was going to happen in the world would happen despite him, maybe, or because of him, maybe —and either way, what happened would be the same. He did not feel out of control; he only felt indifferent. At this moment, with dancers whirling in front of him and the noise of fiddle-and-accordion music echoing in his head, he knew only two things: that he would have a hangover in the morning, and right now he needed to relieve himself.

"Excuse me," he said, thinking he was still sitting beside Bonnie. "Don't leave."

He went out into the vestibule and pushed at the door of the men's room. The door was locked. He pushed again, hit it with his fist, kicked at it.

"Somebody's in there," said a voice behind him.

Marshall turned. An old man in a gray Stetson saluted him and went on into the dance.

"Thank you," Marshall said.

He backed away from the door and leaned against the popcorn machine. The machine was warm and brilliantly lighted; it smelled like butter, and it hummed. The idea of popcorn made his stomach churn.

He walked unsteadily to the rest-room door and rapped at it. "Anybody inside?"

"Hold your water," said a voice.

"I don't know if I can," Marshall said, half-aloud. He went back to lean on the popcorn machine.

The machine impressed him. It was about six feet tall; it had a transparent plastic front so you could see the mounds of golden popcorn inside; it had a slot from which you yanked a paper sack, and a spout where the popcorn poured out.

"What are you standing out here for?" It was Bonnie; she had come to look for him.

"I have to go to the john."

"Well, it's right there."

"Somebody's using it. He's got the door locked."

"Then go outside. Go around the back or something." She took his elbow. "Come on, silly."

"No, hang on. I'll use this."

"Use what?"

He unzipped his Levi's. The popcorn spout was just at urinal height.

"Marshall, no," she said. "Don't do that."

"I can't wait," he said, and then, realizing what he was doing, he started to giggle.

Bonnie left him. The next thing he knew, people were hitting him. Somebody grabbed his collar and pulled him away from the popcorn machine; somebody else punched him in the stomach. His right hand was wet with his own urine. What the hell is the matter with me? Marshall thought, and then he caught a fist on the side of his head and saw a spatter of sparks and fell down.

When he came to, the music had stopped but his head sang with throbbing. His crotch was cold and damp. He felt a sharp pain in the right side of his chest, and his mouth was salty with blood. Bonnie was kneeling beside him.

"You dumb clown," she said.

He turned his head; his neck hurt.

"Every cowboy in the place was hitting on you. Carl says you're lucky they didn't kill you; he says you probably got at least a broken rib and you better count your teeth." She cradled his head in her lap. "They say you got to pay to replace the popcorn machine."

"I will," he said. "I promise I will."

"I can't unriddle you people from out East," Bonnie said gently. "Half what you do is all well and good, and the other half just seems to provoke the worst side of folks."

ROBLEY WILSON, JR., is the author of three earlier story collections: *The Pleasures of Manhood, Living Alone,* and *Dancing for Men,* the winner of the 1982 Drue Heinz Prize. His book of poems, *Kingdoms of the Ordinary,* won the Agnes Lynch Starrett Prize in 1986. He was a 1983–84 Guggenheim Fellow in fiction.